Canon
The Fortuna Dare Society
A Book Club For Men

Rochelle Bradley

DEDICATION

For all the book clubs. Happy reading!

ACKNOWLEDGMENTS

Thank you to the Dayton area WriMos who joined with me during November. I appreciated your companionship. Thank you to my wonderful PA Sara, editor Becky, and my friends and family who encouraged me to keep writing.

A NOTE FROM ROCHELLE

Dear Reader,

Thank you for grabbing book two in the The Fortuna Dare Society series. I loved Jessie's dad admitting he was in a book club in book one of the Fortuna, Texas series and, over time, the Fortuna Dare Society grew in my mind.

I wrote **Brad** and **Canon** during National Novel Writing Month (NaNoWriMo) in November surrounded by many Dayton writers. I was worried that six romance-loving men would be hard to distinguish on the page. They were a hoot, and I enjoyed their witty banter. I hope you will too.

Thanks again, and happy reading!

~Rochelle

CHAPTER ONE

Canon Berns rushed around the kitchen of station house twenty-five, clamoring to clean up before the guys detected the smoke. He used a cereal box to fan the air toward the open window.

It isn't working. Smoke lingered. He was going to catch such hell. He'd only been gone a few minutes to take a dump, and when he returned, the popcorn had caught fire.

The cereal box flopped open, flinging cornflakes over the floor and out the window. He blinked at the mess. Murphy's law had it in for him today.

Throwing the popcorn bag in the sink, he doused it with water. Acrid tendrils wafted heavenward. He scooped up the soggy, burned blob and dropped it into a large black trash bag. He turned the ceiling fans onto high.

Canon groaned. Under the sink, he found Christmas air freshener and debated spraying it. He decided against it, thinking the fresh pine scent mixed with burnt popcorn might smell like a forest fire.

The inside of the ancient microwave could double for a NASA experiment. He sprayed glass cleaner and scrubbed, but it didn't smell clean. The rank odor would assault anyone who opened the door.

Frantic, he whirled, then dug into the pantry. "Ah ha!" he said, spotting a gallon of apple cider vinegar.

Canon mixed water and vinegar in a coffee cup and stuck it in the microwave for five minutes.

A burst of guffaws met his ears. The crew talked with the chief in a conference room.

Canon gnawed his lip while pacing the open kitchen and living space.

A crash on his right startled him. A small black bird hopped on the floor next to a talking Deadpool action figure. The figure's disconnected arm and sword lay beside the body. "My common sense is tingling," it said.

"Great," Canon grumbled. "Why did it have to be the chief's favorite toy?" He picked up the pieces and returned them to the counter.

The bird pecked at the cereal.

Canon approached the bird, but it flew to the top of the refrigerator, streaking the front with poop. He used the push broom to sweep the cereal into a pile. As he collected it in the dustpan and dumped it in the trash bag, he considered shooing the bird with the broom.

When the microwave beeped, he glanced in without opening it. The steam should cleanse the innards. He hoped.

On this day of all days, everything that could go wrong did. *Murphy's Law sucks*. He sighed and hurried past his crew, carrying the trash bag to the dumpster outside.

As he returned, the bird swooped down the hallway, diving into the conference room. "What the hell!" the chief bellowed.

Canon crept past the chaos and back into the kitchen. He wiped the counter and fridge with a lemon scented cleaner and then closed the window.

Canon hoisted his duffel onto his shoulder. "See ya," he called to the guys. He waved, then rushed out the door.

Already behind schedule, Canon glanced at his watch and sighed. He hadn't planned on showering at his apartment, but he had to get the burnt popcorn smell out of his nose and clothes. He took the stairs to the second level two at a time. At the top, he crashed into a petite woman.

Dressed in frumpy sweats and dark-rimmed glasses, she glanced up from the screen of her phone. She gasped and her hazel eyes widened.

"Dude, you bumped off me. Are you all right?" He stabilized her so she wouldn't bounce down the stairs. One minute he had a girl in his arms, all softness and warmth, the next, she pulled away and his arms were empty. *Easy come easy go.*

"Sorry. I'm fine. Thanks," she stammered, a blush blossoming. Her gaze raked his body, then a hint of a grin teased her full lips.

Canon tilted his head, inspecting her. "Are you sure you're all right? You're flushed."

At this, she sucked in a breath and glanced anywhere but his eyes. "Just embarrassed. I'm fine."

"Can I walk you to your door or car? I want to make sure you're safe."

She pressed her lips together and stared at the emblem on his squad T-shirt while pointing to the door across from his.

"Oh. We're neighbors." He lifted his hand in a friendly wave. "Howdy neighbor."

She blinked and stepped closer to her apartment.

He stuck his hand out. "I'm Canon. Nice to meet you."

"I'll be…" She stuck the key in her lock, then, with a curt nod, disappeared inside.

As the door closed, he said, "See you around." The door clicked into place without her saying a word.

"Huh? Must be shy." Canon entered his apartment. He flung garments into the bathroom hamper. "Hey AImee. What's the weather today?" His AI home assistant responded from her little white box on the kitchen counter. "Thank you, AImee."

"You're welcome, Canon. Would you like tomorrow's forecast?" The computerized-feminine voice asked.

"Sure." He twisted the tap and hopped into the water spray. "AImee, can you find me a soulmate?"

"Are you trying to shop for Sole Mate shoes?"

"No." *I wish it was that easy.*

Canon showered, toweled off, dressed, and threw some clothes in a duffle.

As he left, he hollered, "AImee, turn off the light." The kitchen light winked out. He took the stairs three at a time. Driving away, Canon glanced at his apartment to make sure he had turned off the bedroom light and swore his neighbor's blinds shifted.

At the grocery, he filled his coolers with ice and bought the items assigned to him. He'd planned to get everything a day or two before, but Murphy'd had other ideas.

Once on the road, excitement surpassed everything the preceding days had thrown at him. He was over the station, his mysterious neighbor, traffic, renegade birds, and his inability to use a microwave. To heck with it all. He was going on an adventure. He was entering the world of fiction with his book club friends.

CHAPTER TWO

CANON TURNED INTO THE DOUBLE D ranch's drive. He slowed as Josiah Barnes, the ranch foreman, walked toward his truck.

"Looks like you're a little late to the party," Josiah said with a smile.

"Only fashionably so," Canon replied, smiling.

Josiah pointed in the barn's direction. "Drive past the barn and turn right. You'll see a lane. Follow the tracks. They'll have a large fire going by this time. I'm glad they'll have a representative there from the firehouse."

"I always carry my handy-dandy extinguisher to a bonfire in case things get out of hand," Canon said.

"Is it something special?" Josiah's curiosity peaked.

"Some think so," Canon laughed. "I pee on the fire to put it out."

Josiah shook his head. "I'm glad I didn't ask you to show me." He waved Canon on, still shaking his head.

Canon bumped over the primitive road, the shocks working overtime. The sunlight had hung on long enough for him to see the pillar of smoke in the distance. The tent he spotted looked lopsided. He'd have to help them fix it or else it could slip in the night and scare the bejesus out of them.

He turned off the ignition and pushed open the door. Brad Davidson, B.J. Johnson, and Jasen DeLay all approached. By the time Canon had lowered his pickup's gate and climbed in the bed, the men had caught up to him. "Howdy y'all. I've got coolers with beer." He pulled the blue cooler forward.

"Grab a handle," B.J. ordered Jasen. Each man took a handle and carried it toward the fire.

Canon admired B.J. and Jasen. In their early thirties, both men had successful careers. One was the supervisor of a property management company and the other was Fortuna's honorable mayor.

"Need help?" Brad asked, "Can I carry that, son?"

Grateful, Canon smiled. He'd packed the cooler full and didn't know if Brad could handle the weight.

Brad owned the Big Deal ranch and might have been a tough cowboy at one time, but now he was older and a paper pusher. The oldest of the book club members, Brad had to be close to a hundred. Although, maybe not, because his daughter was thirty.

"Thanks Brad, but I've got it." Canon took both handles and hoisted it. It was heavy, but nothing different from what he carried at the station. Nothing like the weight of his gear.

B.J. and Jasen joined Parker Ford and Forrest Greene in a ring of chairs around a fire pit. Parker stirred a large kettle suspended over the fire.

Canon followed B.J. and Jasen, setting his cooler next

to theirs. B.J. and Jasen looked winded, but it could have been from the tug of war he saw them playing with the cooler.

The heavenly aroma of chili hung in the air. Canon's stomach rumbled.

"Now that we're all here—" the mayor started.

"What's the status of the food?" *Oh God, I interrupted the mayor*. Canon quickly lifted the lid of the cooler and grabbed a bottle of beer. He offered it to Brad.

"Age before beauty," BJ teased, crossing his arms.

Brad's bristly mustache twitched with a smile. "I've earned it, you whipper-snapper." Brad twisted off the cap. He settled in a seat next to Forrest and raised the longneck.

Canon quickly handed out bottles to everyone who wanted one. They all raised their beverages.

"To my mother Undine Love-Davidson and her freakish book hoarding tendencies. May the good Lord give her an enormous mansion with thousands of books," Brad clicked Forrest's water bottle, then Canon's beer.

"Here, here," Canon said.

Parker returned to the kettle and stirred.

"Now that we're all here—" Jasen started again, his eyes narrowing at Canon.

Canon shrunk back and swallowed.

Parker sniffed the kettle, closed his eyes and said, "Soups on."

Canon jumped up. "Awesome! What can I do to help?"

"Get the fixin's out of the cooler," Parker ordered, pointing to a small red cooler while he began pulling bowls out of a canvas bag. Brad spooned the chili into his bowl first and topped it with peppers. He smiled and sighed. It was a good sign.

Once Canon had his, he ladled a large spoonful into his mouth. He savored the sting of the spice. Parker's was the best chili he'd ever had, next to Grammie Nan's. He kept spooning mouthfuls in.

"Too hot for you?" Jasen asked.

Canon glanced over to B.J. He switched from blowing on his bowl to gulping his beer.

Jasen took his first spoonful while B.J. glowered at him. "God, Parker, this is fabulous. Holy cow."

"Mm-hmm," Canon hummed, nodding his head and holding his empty bowl out for more.

"Damn. How did you eat that so fast?" B.J. asked.

"He's not a pansy like you." Forrest took a large bite.

B.J. must have taken it as a challenge because he took a large spoonful. Everybody in Fortuna knew B.J. didn't back down from challenges or dares. He was the one who'd started the romance reading fad in town. He'd accepted a dare to read a romance novel and found he loved them. Soon he dared other men and voilà—book club.

B.J.'s face grew red as he moved the food from one cheek to another. He swallowed, then lifted the beer bottle to his lips and chugged it until it was empty. Sweat beaded on his brow.

Everyone laughed. Parker finally sat to eat and dived in with a satisfied smile.

Canon took a trash bag and opened it. "Put your empty bottles and bowls in here." He collected the group's garbage. He'd lock it in the truck's cab to keep unwanted critters away.

Parker lifted the lid on a container. Inside sat the most perfect chocolate chip cookies Canon had ever seen. They looked plastic and too good to eat.

"Lisa made these special for y'all. I hope you don't like them, so there's more for me." Parker passed the plate. Canon took one and devoured ti.

Jasen took a cookie, then sampled it. His eyes rolled back, and he moaned.

"Geez, Jasen, you eat too much processed food," Forrest said, then nibbled the cookie and moaned.

"I know, right?" Canon said, swiping another cookie as the plate passed back.

"Please give Lisa my compliments. These are excellent." Brad popped the last bite into his mouth.

Parker smiled and nodded. "I'll be sure to tell her."

"How are you two doing?" Forrest asked, wiping crumbs from his face.

Canon's gaze volleyed from Forrest to Parker. Parker and Lisa Ford were quite a pair. He knew two things about the couple. One was that they used to fight all the time. He knew this firsthand from a yelling match he'd witnessed in Hammered, the local restaurant. The second was something he was glad he didn't witness. Parker had gotten caught by the police while trying to act out a favorite romance novel hero. Unfortunately for him, he was sans clothes when the officers found him.

The book fad had elevated public fighters to public lovers, and he'd heard women wish their man was more like Parker Ford.

Forrest was married, too. He and his wife, Ivy, had a little girl. But Forrest hadn't made it to Parker's level of notoriety. He might have attempted things, but his wife worked for the Fortuna police as a dispatcher, and it probably wouldn't look good if she or her husband were arrested.

"Well," Parker started, his round cheeks turned pink, "She's good. She recently discovered the books at city hall."

"Oh God," Jasen groaned, covering his face.

Forrest leaned forward, appearing intrigued. "Ivy has asked about the stash of books, too. Any luck?"

Parker chuckled, leaned back, and crossed his arms over his broad chest. "A little. My suggestion is: let her pick something."

Jasen put his arms out like someone was safe at home plate. "I know you don't believe me, but just for the record, those novels are not in my office. I'll state once again I didn't ask to have a bookshelf or the BDSM books placed there." He threw B.J. the stink eye.

"Says you." B.J. smirked and leaned back with crossed arms.

Jasen furrowed his brow and puckered his lips, like he

smelled something rank. He shot his hand out and pushed the corner of B.J.'s folding chair next to his shoulder. B.J. teetered with his arms and legs flailing. The chair tipped, and he landed in a plume of dust with his feet in the air.

Canon bit his tongue to keep from laughing.

B.J. jumped to his feet with balled fists, a red vein bulging on his forehead.

Jasen ignored B.J. and popped another cookie into his mouth. Canon held his breath, waiting to see if the men would fight.

Brad pointed to B.J.'s chair, and B.J. took the hint and righted it, then sat. "What are we going to read next?"

Canon admired Brad's even-tempered response. He could've gotten mad when the grown men acted like stupid kids. Nice redirect.

Forrest glanced up at the stars, stroking his ginger beard.

"How about historical?" Jasen suggested.

B.J. laughed. "Bodice rippers."

"You like them," Jasen said with a smirk.

"Yes, you do B.J." Forrest said. "I've seen them at your office."

B.J. shrugged. "I read them all. I don't discriminate."

A few days ago in Nockerville, Canon had picked up a romance set in Montana. He'd read the first few chapters and liked it. The author had two series with several books and would be a great read for the book club. "We could do western romance, but somewhere new, like Montana or Colorado."

"I'll make a list." Jasen opened a notebook and began writing. "We can read them all, eventually."

"Cool. I liked *Sweet Vengeance*. It had vampires, sorcerers, and werewolves. Why don't we do werewolves?" Canon raised his arms and curled his fingers like claws. "Aah-oo," he howled.

Forrest rolled his eyes. "Can we take a break from paranormal for a while? How about romantic comedy? Something in a small town, maybe."

"You just want something easy to act out," Parker teased.

Forrest's eyes widened, and he turned bright red.

"Hot damn, Parker is right!" B.J. clapped his hands together, then he jumped up. He started pacing within the circle of chairs.

"Oh crap," Brad said as he met Jasen's gaze.

Canon watched B.J. move. His brow was crinkled as he mulled something over. After a few minutes, he stopped, then turned to face them, jabbing a finger into the air. "I have an idea."

"Here it comes," Jasen muttered with pen poised.

B.J. ignored him and said, "Let's draw."

As far as Canon could tell, Jasen was the only man with a pen. "I don't have a pencil."

"No you goof. Like this..." B.J. turned to Jasen. "Can I use your notebook?" With a nod, Jasen handed it over. B.J. tore six sheets out, then handed it back.

He ripped the sheets in thirds, then handed each man three pieces. "On the top paper list a setting. Like a city, the mountains, or a diner. Whatever. Think where you'd like to read."

B.J. handed the pen to Forrest. He scribbled his place, then passed the pen to Brad.

When the men had finished, B.J. asked, "Brad, may I borrow your cowboy hat?" The men folded the slips of paper and added them to the hat.

"Draw one and make sure it isn't yours. Keep what you receive to yourself. Tuck it in your chair's cup holder."

Canon reached in and chose a slip of paper.

"Now think of a subgenre you'd like to read or act out." B.J. wiggled his brows, earning a few chuckles. "I guess it could be a common trope, like the secret baby or friends to lovers."

Once more, the pen circled the group, then the men dropped their ideas into the hat.

B.J. shook Brad's hat, then offered him first dibs. He selected a paper.

After they each had picked a subgenre, B.J. said, "Now select a character. Not someone specific, but like a clown or shop owner."

Canon chuckled, then wrote something he hoped Forrest would get. He threw his paper in the pot. When it was his turn, he drew a character.

"Jasen, write these down," B.J. ordered.

Jasen nodded with pen poised.

The silence stretched. Forrest mouthed something to Brad that Canon didn't catch. Brad shrugged and glanced at the fire.

Canon liked the idea of randomly picking reading topics. It was a fresh idea.

"Look at your paper," B.J. smirked and pointed to Forrest. "I dare you to act these out with your wife. And you," he said, pointing to Parker. "The rest of us need to find someone."

Brad and Jasen shared a look. Both were widowers. They'd lost their wives in tragic accidents.

The image of Canon's frumpy neighbor in his arms popped into his head. He shook it away. "I, uh," Canon stuttered. "I don't have a girlfriend."

"Are you afraid of a little dare?" B.J. taunted.

"Neither do you," Jasen said to B.J.

B.J.'s brows rose. "Don't worry, I'm looking forward to dressing up like …" He shuffled his papers and croaked, "A prince."

Canon sucked in a breath and stymied his laughter, but Forrest had no such control.

"Charming," Jasen teased.

"Not." Parker snorted.

"What's your trope?" Canon leaned forward.

B.J. unfolded a second paper. "MC. What the hell is MC?"

"Motorcycle club." Canon smirked.

"You get to be a royal bad boy," Brad said.

"More like a royal pain in the ass," Jasen grinned.

"Who likes leather," Parker added. "You might want to visit Jasen's bookshelf for ideas." He winked.

"What's your setting B.J.?" Canon asked.

"Haunted coffee shop." B.J. shook his head. "A coffee shop would be easy enough but haunted? How the hell am I going to pull that off?"

Canon laughed. He'd like to see him figure it out, too. "Are you afraid of your own dare?"

B.J. snarled and dropped into his seat. He glowered at the fire.

"Listen, son," Brad started, catching everyone's undivided attention. "You could be a singer formally known as Prince imitator who drives a Harley and sings haunting melodies at hipster coffee shops."

"Have you heard B.J. sing?" Forrest asked. "I have at church. It would be haunting, all right. It'd scare the shiznack out of them."

"Ha Ha." B.J. rubbed his chin. "I like Brad's interpretation. I suppose we can manipulate our choices as long as they can be described in the original terminology. What did you get Brad?"

Brad smoothed the folds out of his papers as he read, "Alien, fairytale, and library."

Jasen hastily jotted it down.

Parker offered, "Mine are a dancer, a billionaire with a hidden past, and Scotland. I think Lisa will like the kilt."

"Anyone want to switch?" Forrest asked, waving his slips of paper.

"No switching," B.J. said, looking like the devil.

"This is such bull-crap." Forrest scowled at B.J., then sighed. "A vampire mystery at a club."

"That bites," Parker teased.

Forrest had lamented reading vampires, and that's why Canon threw the blood sucker into the hat. He bit his tongue to hide his pleasure.

"What do you have, Canon?" Parker asked.

With all eyes on him, he heated. "My character has to be a superhero, set in the past, on a train."

"That's easy." Brad met his eyes. "The Lone Ranger. You can skip the tights."

B.J. opened the drinks cooler and offered everyone another round. Canon accepted one and smiled. Even though he was the youngest member of the group, they treated him with respect and he didn't feel like a kid. Most of the time.

The only one not to reveal his dare was, "Jasen?" B.J. beat Canon to asking.

Jasen sighed. "I have no clue how to pull this off. A cowboy fantasy in the theatre."

"Why?" Canon asked, leaning forward.

"The main reason is I don't have a wife, girlfriend or even someone I'd remotely want to take to coffee, let alone cos-play with." Jasen frowned and looked away.

"I don't either," Brad said, sympathizing.

"That's not true, Brad." B.J. said, flashing a wily smile.

Brad's mouth dropped open, but he didn't utter a word.

"For once, I agree with B.J." Jasen raised his bottle.

One member of their book club was missing. The

expert in all things bookish and feminine. Those happened to be Brad's words about Fortuna's librarian: Ophelia Cox. She'd joined the club to keep them on task and offer a woman's point of view. He'd learned a lot about plots, characterization, and whatnot. Canon had noticed she admired Brad, but maybe it was more.

"Are you guys talking about Ms. Ophelia?" Canon glanced from B.J. and Jasen to Brad.

"Yes, Ophelia." B.J. said scrutinizing Brad. "I seem to recall she contacts you first when we need to change a time. She always gushes about how sexy mustaches are, too."

Canon had always envied Brad's bushy mustache. He reminded Canon of Sam Elliot.

Brad touched his whiskers with a hint of a grin.

"I've got one, so does Jasen," Forrest said, stroking his beard.

"Dude. You do not have a mustache. You have a beard. A long, bushy, probably can find last week's food stored in it, beard. And Jasen's isn't really a beard, or is it? It's like three days' growth," Canon said.

"I call it lazy," B.J. said.

"It is," Jasen admitted. "Until I need to trim it."

They compared facial hair care techniques and Canon zoned out. Mostly because he couldn't grow a full beard. When he let it grow, his face looked like a molting chicken.

Canon thought about the dare. The superhero part would be easy—but set in the past on a train? He scratched his patchy five o'clock shadow.

"Your beard care is fascinating, Jasen, but how about we pick books? Then we can read awhile before we retire," Brad offered.

Canon sat up. "Where are the books?"

"Better yet, how can we retire if there's only one tent?" Parker posed. "I mean, I like all y'all all right, but I'm not fixin' to bunk with the five of you."

Jasen and B.J. shared a look.

"Oh." Canon stood. "Can I put the other tents up?" He picked up the pack before anyone could reply.

"Sure, knock yourself out," B.J. said.

Canon had always enjoyed putting tents together. He and his cousins were scouts, and they used to race to see who could put them up the fastest. The tent he pulled out of the bag was familiar because it was his. He put the poles together, then placed them into the slots. Like a puzzle. Within a few minutes, he'd completed the task.

"How the hell did you do that?" B.J. asked, sitting up wide-eyed.

"I was a scout. Plus, this one was mine." Canon couldn't help but grin. "Where are the books?"

Parker brought the totes of books near enough to the firelight so the men could see. "There are aliens and spaceships in these three." Canon looked up.

"Sci-fi?" Parker glanced at Forrest, who nodded. "Okay?"

With everyone in agreement, they passed the books around, reading the backs until everyone had picked one.

Next week they would switch, but tonight Canon was sure he'd picked a good one. His fingers itched to open it.

Brad and Canon shared a tent. Canon quickly undressed and slid on a pair of basketball shorts. He laid on his sleeping bag and began reading while Brad pulled off his boots and jeans.

The humanoid alien was naked in the first chapter and, "Oh my." Canon blinked at Brad. "This one is going to be saucy. Awesome."

Canon turned his attention back to the book and read three chapters before dousing the lantern.

CHAPTER THREE

THE CAMPING WEEKEND HAD WIPED Canon out. He blinked dry eyes, blaming it on the reading and the campfire smoke.

The chili he had feasted on hadn't agreed with him. Luckily, he'd taken Monday off.

"Hey, AImee, what time does Fu King Wok close?"

"Eleven o'clock, Canon," AImee replied, its circular rim glowing neon green. "Would you like to know tomorrow's weather?"

"No."

"Okay, Canon."

"Looks like I'm going to Fu King Wok." He had a slight addiction to crab Rangoon.

When Canon returned home, his petite neighbor rounded the corner, trotting down the stairs. This time, they only *nearly* collided. She wore her uniform of an over-sized shirt and glasses. Her brown hair topped her head in a sloppy but sexy bun.

He wasn't sure why he noticed, but her purple-painted toenails peeked out of her athletic sandals.

"Hi there," Canon greeted with a large grin.

Her face turned red, but she said, "Hi."

"I'm Canon." He shifted the bag of food to his other hand.

"I know." She grabbed her purse strap and stepped back.

"I don't bite," he promised with a wink, holding his hand out.

"Oh." The blush on her face deepened, and she took his hand in a quick but firm handshake. "Gotta go."

"Okie-dokey." Canon stepped aside, and she rushed down the steps. He glanced at her name on her mail slot. "See you, Ms. Batch."

She spun around fast, a smirk on her full lips. "What did you say?"

Canon swallowed. "See you later."

"No, you butchered my name."

"Batch?"

She giggled, and the smile made her face light up. "It's Bach."

Butterflies took flight in his stomach. "As in J.S.?" Canon asked, tilting his head.

"J.S.?"

"Johann Sebastian, the composer."

Her mouth fell open for a moment, then she nodded, blinked twice, and raised her hand. "Bye."

Canon watched her flee to her car and drive off. He found her oddness amusing, and he doubled down on his determination to befriend her.

Canon stepped into the dark room. "AImee, turn on the light." With a chime, the light clicked on.

He lounged on the brown leather sofa, feasting on crab Rangoon and General Tso's chicken. But his apartment was too quiet, and he missed the noise of the station house and his book club.

"AImee play eighties music."

"Playing your eighties playlist." Music filled the room. Between mouthfuls he sang along, filling the quiet.

After dinner, Canon reached for the romance he'd found on the bookshelf at the station. A regency historical—what Forrest called a bodice ripper. The mystery intrigued Canon as well as the use of the word quit. People like to quit rooms. "If they quit a room, did they ever go back to it?"

Six chapters later, he hankered for something sweet. Jumping to his feet, he strode to the kitchen and pulled open the freezer. He opened the container of ice cream. Except for two spoonfuls, the ice cream was gone. He sighed, having on one to blame except himself.

"Looks like I'm going to the store."

Grabbing the key fob from the counter, he exited the apartment.

Blaring music assaulted him. Canon shook his head. He tried to be a good neighbor and not make noise others might hear. Families lived in the complex and little ones had bedtimes.

A breeze blew, stirring debris on the landing. Dry grass clippings swirled. The small landing was dark as he closed the door. His apartment complex had buildings lined in a row. Canon's was in the center building.

Once in the parking lot, he learning the offending party was in the apartment adjacent to Ms. Bach's. They had strung lights on the small wooden balcony where three people stood smoking. Light and music spilled out of the open sliding glass door.

Ms. Bach probably wouldn't like the bass pumping near her headboard. He glanced around for her Civic.

Vehicles filled the lot, more parking as he watched. He sighed, the need for ice cream overcoming his fear of losing his primo parking spot.

At Wertz Grocery he bought three gallons of ice cream, Fudgesicles and a six-pack of Mother's Milk beer from Nockerville.

Canon had to park far from his apartment, next to the dumpster. The music was louder than before. Police arrived with flashing lights. As he took the steps, a Fortuna officer headed for the parallel set of stairs leading to the troublemakers.

Once inside his apartment, the loud music disappeared, save for the thumping bass. He kicked off his shoes, and the floor vibrated. Canon unwrapped a fudge pop and picked up the romance again. After an overflowing bowl of butter pecan, which took longer to fill than eat, he shimmied out of his pants and shirt, then went to bed.

His bedroom was further from the noise of the party and if he closed the door and asked AImee to play rain sounds, Canon could pretend to be camping away from home. He stretched his long legs and leaned back with a sigh. Thoughts of the bodice ripper's hero and heroine frolicking in the English countryside fluttered through his mind.

The England and Scotland period stories were nice, but he needed to reference more modern tales for his dare. Something from the turn of the twentieth century. Would the 1940s count as historical?

How would a man have dressed for everyday life? Probably a suit and tie. He placed his hands behind his head and closed his eyes, imagining himself in a zoot suit.

How would frumpy Ms. Bach have dressed? A dress with a flattering neckline, pearls, and stockings. Did she even have a chest to flatter? Who'd ever know with the over-sized sweatshirts she always wore?

It wasn't completely true. When he'd ran into her, he'd bumped into *all* of her.

He rolled over to his side, willing his neighbor out of his mind, yet she stubbornly hung around, pestering him. Everyone always liked him. Her constant fear of him plagued Canon.

She was a tiny thing. Maybe she'd been abused. Anger surged, and he rolled to his other side.

"Stupid," he muttered. "She's probably smart enough to be careful around overly friendly strangers."

Next time he saw her, he would nod and continue on his way. Hopefully, he'd seem less of a creeper.

Canon stretched and turned over again. "AImee, turn on storm sounds." Thunder rolled and rain pattered, but the bass still thumped. "AImee, volume up."

CHAPTER FOUR

Canon bolted upright in bed. His heart hammered and chest heaved. It was pitch black. Rain pelted the windows and thunder rumbled in the distance.

Then he remembered. "AImee stop."

The smoke detector screeched. He coughed and his throat burned. Sirens wailed, drawing nearer by the second.

"Oh, shit." He scrambled out of bed, tripping on the blanket. He found his footing and said, "AImee, turn on the light."

The light illuminated a wisp of smoke swirling near the ceiling.

"Oh shit, oh shit, oh shit."

Threading his legs through a pair of basketball shorts, Canon grabbed his wallet and keys. He threw them into a basket of clean clothes. With the basket on his hip, he felt the front door. It wasn't hot, so he opened it.

All in pajamas, a family from the third floor rushed past in a panic. A little girl clung to a stuffed animal. "Stay together. Hold Mark's hand. Remember what we said if we get separated? Who's got the cat?"

Canon swallowed and let the people pass. The door

across the way remained closed. He hoped Ms. Bach had already fled.

Smoke hung in the air and he covered his nose with his arm. The glass globe overhead flickered, then winked off. Canon blinked, and with his empty hand, grabbed the railing.

An orange glow reflected off windshields. Like a dummy, he had forgotten shoes. He stepped gingerly down the cool slabbed stairs until he reached the grass. He turned toward the building.

Canon gasped. The party apartment was on fire. Flames escaped the windows on the second and licked the third floor. Heat dried his eyes as he stared, mesmerized. A woman nudged his arm as she cradled her child.

Snapped out of his daze, Canon took off in a brisk walk toward his truck. He opened the door and set his basket on the seat. Rummaging through his clothes, he found a fire department T-shirt and slipped it on. On the floor in the back were his dirty boots from the book club camp out. He stepped into them and hurried toward station twenty-five's trucks.

Canon's station mates sprayed the building. He approached the chief. "Hey, can I help?" Canon asked.

The chief wiped his face with a gloved hand, inspecting him head to boots. "Not in those duds. Where'd you come from?"

"I live there," He pointed to the next landing.

"Get the people to move to the other side of the lot. Preferably on the grass near the road. Nockerville is sending an engine over." He nodded, then hurried to the radio.

Canon started with a couple nearest to the building. Tears glistened on the woman's cheeks. "Hi, I work for the Fortuna fire department. The chief asked me to move everyone to the other area on the far side of the parking lot."

He continued to work closer toward his building. All his neighbors were present except the frumpy Bach girl. Canon spun, checking for her Honda. It was in the parking lot. His breath accelerated as he ran from crowd to crowd calling, "Ms. Bach."

Canon's gut clenched. He couldn't find the Bach babe, and she had to be home. He ran toward the building, skirting across the parking lot, dodging vehicles and men.

The second engine arrived, wailing.

The flames sparked the roof of the building next to his frumpy neighbor's apartment. A fire wall separated them, but heat anything hot enough, and it will burn.

Canon swallowed and ran for her door. He knocked. The power was out, so ringing the bell wouldn't work. He pounded with his fist. "Come on, wake up!"

He kicked next. He only listened for a moment before trying to ram it with his shoulder. It gave a little, but the chain latch caught. He tried again, and the mechanism jerked out of the doorjamb. Filled with smoke, the living space was uncomfortably warm. He raised his shirt over his nose and moved fast. The girl wasn't on the sofa, so he continued to the bedroom. Her floor plan mirrored his.

The bedroom door was closed. It was warm to the touch, but not super heated. Twisting the knob, a great bellow of smoke wafted out. In the smoky blackness, Canon couldn't see. Coughing, he felt for the bed. In the center, he felt a body. She coughed, then groaned. He scooped her up as fire sprang to life in the far corner of the ceiling.

"Oh, hell."

With Ms. Bach over his shoulder, he hurried to the door. He tripped over something and landed on his knees.

Her purse! He took the handle and continued to the door. His eyes watered, and he struggled to put one foot in front of the other.

Once down the steps, he continued to an ambulance. "She needs help. I found her in a smoke-filled room."

Canon lowered her to the gurney. When the EMT rolled her onto her back, Canon gasped. The long, dark-haired beauty with the ash smeared face was unfamiliar to him. She wore a turquoise spaghetti strap tank top that clung to her curves and short pjs that showed off toned legs.

God, had he rescued a different girl? Was frumpy still in there?

The girl coughed and opened her round eyes. Her gaze traveled around, first hitting the man who worked on her, taking her blood pressure. Then to the other who was talking to her, telling her she's all right. Her gaze settled last on Canon and widened.

"What's going on?" she asked in a scratchy voice. She

coughed again.

"The apartment building is on fire." Canon glanced back at her apartment. Flames danced in the bedroom window. If he hadn't sought her out, she would have died. He rubbed his face, breathing hard.

She coughed.

"Hey Berns, what's your girlfriend's name?"

She sucked in a breath and shook her head. "Albie Bach," she wheezed.

"Canon, you did real good rescuing this little lady," the EMT said as he removed the blood pressure cuff.

"I only did what's right, Jonas," Canon said, glancing down at his boots.

"Let's get her loaded and go," Jonas said, strapping her to the gurney.

"Wait." Albie's hand shot out and clasped Canon's. "My cat."

Canon frowned and stepped toward the building. Jonas stepped in his way. "No way, man, you can't go back. It's suicide."

Flames engulfed her fabric headboard and the walls. If the cat was in there, he was toast. Literally. Tears pricked his eyes. He turned back to Albie and shook his head.

"No." She sat up and twisted toward the building. Glimpsing the fire for the first time, she shrieked. "Oh, my God. My apartment. My stuff."

Her hands covered her face, and she gave in to tears. Canon put a hand on her shoulder and watched through

Albie's sliding glass doors as the flames spread into the living room.

Canon squeezed her shoulder, and her head tipped in his direction. "I didn't close the door. Maybe your kitty escaped."

She nodded, then buried her face in his shirt. He patted her back and started to cough.

Jonas insisted Canon come to the hospital. He nodded and followed in his truck. If the Fortuna fire fighters didn't get the blaze under control soon, then he'd lose everything, like Albie.

On the drive to Nockerville Memorial Hospital, Canon made a call. "Hi Grammie," he started.

"Oh, honey, I heard about your apartment complex. I've been praying you'd be safe and call me." Just the sound of her warm, loving voice brought the emotion to the surface. He blinked it away.

"How did you…?"

"The news. It looks bad. Is it near your place?"

"It started in a building down from mine, but as I left, it was consuming my neighbor's apartment. It might have taken her cat."

"Oh, that's a shame."

"I grabbed a basket of clothes, my wallet and keys, but my neighbor isn't as fortunate." Canon turned the wheel, exiting the highway.

"Why is that?" she asked.

"She was asleep, and I had to break in and rescue her. She has only the clothes she was wearing."

"Poor thing. No home. No personal items and no pet."

"She'll need a place to stay." He rubbed his face. "I might need a place to stay, too."

CHAPTER FIVE

LOOKING IN THE MIRROR AS Canon parked, his dark-streaked face surprised him. He attempted to rub the grime away, but his sooty knuckles made it worse.

He sighed, locking the truck. Canon hurried to the emergency entrance where the EMTs had left Albie.

He held his breath when he peeked around the curtain. Albie stared at the ceiling with a white blanket pulled to her chin. An ER nurse asked her questions.

"And how does it make you feel?" The nurse clicked and unclicked her ink pen.

"Hot." Albie shifted her gaze to the nurse. She lowered the blanket and waved her hand to cool herself.

Canon smiled as relief rolled over him. Albie seemed unharmed and breathing fine.

"And bothered?" The nurse's tweezed-to-hell brows rose.

"Well…" Albie grimaced as her face reddened. "Yes. I guess. But mostly bothered about me not having the guts to—"

Canon cleared his throat, catching the women's attention. He offered a small smile, hoping Albie wouldn't want him to leave.

"Hello there, and you are?" the nurse asked.

"I'm Ms. Bach's neighbor," Canon stated, stepping inside the curtain.

The nurse scanned his body from top to bottom with a smirk. She turned to Albie. "I see what you mean by B'SHOAF. Yes, ma'am." She wiggled her brows.

Albie groaned, turning crimson. She pulled the blanket over her face except for her wide eyes.

Canon glanced from one woman to the other. "What's a SHOAF?"

"You." The nurse chuckled.

"It's an acronym," Albie said, lowering the blanket. "Each letter stands for something."

"I know what an acronym is. I'm glad I'm not a PITA."

The nurse snorted. "Me too, or you'd have to wait outside."

"I don't know that one." Albie crinkled her nose as if thinking.

Canon couldn't help grinning and moved a few steps closer. With her dark hair fanned out on the crisp white pillow, she didn't appear like the frail girl from before. He swallowed. "It means pain in the ass."

"Oh." She giggled.

"So SHOAF?"

"It's B'SHOAF. There's a B." She glanced down at her fingers and picked a cuticle. "A few weeks ago, my sister asked who you were, and I didn't know your name. I told her B'SHOAF. It was before we kinda met, and you told me your first name." She blinked hazel eyes at him. A lopsided grin formed, and Canon resisted the urge to touch her lips.

"It means 'big, sexy hunk of a firefighter.' B'SHOAF." She offered a weak shrug.

Canon warmed, and his heart raced. She thought he was a sexy hunk. He glanced down at his boots, noticing one was untied. "It's not the worst nickname I've been given. Thanks. You made my day." He tipped his head, then stepped closer to the bed and stuck out his hand. "I'm Canon Berns."

She took his hand; his hand swallowed hers. "I'm Albie."

"Albie Bach? Are you named after the Schwarzenegger movie?" He tried to swallow a laugh.

A full smile blossomed on her face, transforming her from a skittish girl to a confident woman. "No. Actually, I'm named after my Grandma Alberta, but she went by Bertie. My dad didn't think I looked like an Alberta, and my brother couldn't say it. He could say Albie, so it stuck."

She tilted her head and asked, "Are you Canon because you had a big head when you were born?"

"Among other things, but, yeah, you nailed it," he laughed.

Her mouth fell open, then she snapped it shut and hugged herself. Goosebumps peppered her sleeveless arms.

Canon rubbed his chest and then lifted his arm,

holding one of his shirts. "Here, Albie," he said, trying her name.

Her eyes narrowed for a brief second, then she smiled and took the offering. She opened the wadded garment, then slipped it over her head. As the navy squad shirt fell over her thin frame, she sighed. "Thank you."

"I know how you like to wear over-sized items. And you looked cold." Canon shrugged.

She lifted the shirt to her nose and sniffed. "Mmm. It smells like clean laundry. So much better than the smoky smell that's stuck in my nose." She inhaled deeply, then began to cough. And cough. Her face turned red and her eyes watered.

"Can't—" she wheezed, then coughed. "Breathe."

The nurse had already moved. She lowered the oxygen tube and fit it to Albie's face. She tried to calm Albie and wiped her running eyes and nose. Albie fisted the blanket and glanced up at him.

Canon knew what panic looked like. He'd seen it many times. The more she freaked out, the harder it would be to get the proper amount of oxygen. Not enough oxygen made it hard to think.

He put a hand on her arm. "Albie, you are fine. Look at me." When she met his gaze, he continued. "Hold my hand. You are not alone. I won't leave you. Now close your eyes and listen to my voice."

Her eyes fluttered shut, and he squeezed her tiny hand gently. The nurse nodded to him.

"Try to relax. Stretch your legs out and flex your toes.

Point them toward the wall." He paused, watching her feet move under the blanket. "Now point them to the ceiling." Getting her to focus on other things distracted her from her anxiety about breathing.

"Good. Can you raise each leg, one at a time, like a flutter kick?"

Albie's breathing regulated, and the nurse removed the oxygen. "I'm going to draw on the back of your hand. Try to guess what it is?"

"Ok," she said, cracking one eyelid to glance at him.

He moved his finger over her soft skin, making gooseflesh appear on her arm again. "What is it?"

"An eight?"

He started over. "This line is straight."

"Oh, a B then."

"You got it."

She smiled and hissed. "Yes!"

Canon chuckled, glad the game was working. He traced a new letter.

"S," she said.

"Uh huh, try this one." Her brow crinkled as his finger moved.

"H," she guessed.

He continued with, "O."

The next few, she guessed correctly. A and F.

Canon paused and winked at the nurse, who asked, "What's it spell?"

"BSHOAF. Oh!" Albie giggled. She glanced up at him through thick lashes, and he winked at her.

"Honestly, that's the best compliment I've had." His face heated, and he had to be as red as a station twenty-five truck.

Albie clenched the blanket. "You must get complimented all the time by women."

"Nah," he said, sitting on the edge of the bed. "I don't have time for women. Between both jobs and a book club I'm in, there isn't much time for friends, let alone dating. The only woman in my life is my Grammie Nan."

"Book club." Albie tilted her head and studied him. "So, you're one of those guys."

Canon rubbed the back of his head and glanced toward the door. "Um, I guess so."

"So, what type of books do you like to read?" She asked in a curious tone.

Canon faced her again. "Romance."

"Seriously?" She bit her lip, hiding a smile.

"Why not? There are seven of us in the group. Six of us are men."

"Romance reading men." She made a funny noise. "I'd heard about it, but I refused to believe it."

"You haven't been in town long."

She sighed. "Looks like I won't be staying either."

"It'll all work out. Speaking of which, Grammie Nan has a duplex and said you are welcome to crash on the unoccupied side until you figure out where to go next." Canon couldn't meet her eyes. She didn't respond, but squeezed his hand. He gathered his courage and glanced at Albie.

"Wow." She tilted her head. "You're sweet."

Canon felt hot all over and shrugged.

"We'll see," Albie said, closing her eyes. Canon rubbed her hand and watched over her as she slept.

CHAPTER SIX

CANON OPENED THE DOOR TO the duplex. "Grammie, we're here."

"Come on in the kitchen," Grammie said. "I'm fixin' dinner."

Barefoot and in her pajamas, Albie followed him into the living room. Felix, Grammie's black cat, peered up from the oval braided rug on the floor. Not impressed with the guests, Felix rolled over.

The familiar scent of Grammie's home washed nostalgia over Canon, and he sighed. He had so many wonderful memories from the living room alone. On the floral print sofa, he'd heard many stories and shed just as many tears.

The white mantel held pottery knickknacks he'd made in elementary school. He couldn't recall what the colorful blobs were or when he'd made them, but Grammie knew and had a story for each.

"Mm, that smells good," Albie said. She hadn't moved from the doorway.

Canon returned to her and offered his hand. She tentatively took it, smiling at him.

"My Grammie is the best cook," he boasted, happy to

put the statement to the test.

Canon moved slowly to accommodate Albie's shuffle, following the humming. He made it to the doorway of the kitchen and paused when he heard Albie's soft gasp. Her breath fanned the back of his arm and tickled. He chuckled at her expression—the wide-eyes and open mouth.

Grammie was an American of African descent, and Canon may have forgotten to mention it. That kind of detail didn't matter, or rather, he didn't see it anymore. People either were or they weren't. They were kind, or they weren't. They were generous, or they weren't.

Grammie was five-feet if she had her heels on and a hundred pounds dripping wet. Canon liked to lift her when he hugged her. She'd squeal, offering some ailment as an excuse. "You're going to hurt your back," she'd say. If he didn't promptly return her to her feet, she playfully whacked him on the top of his head with whatever she had in her hand, like a spatula or newspaper.

Today she was rolling dough. He wouldn't grab her until she was far away from the rolling pin.

Without looking toward them, Grammie said, "Canon, what did I say about lurking?" She turned on the water and washed her hands.

He stepped into the room. "No lurking in the doorways. Come in or get out."

"Yes sir," she glanced up with a huge grin. "I'm glad you chose to come in." She trained her gaze on Albie. "Welcome, sweetheart." She opened her arms.

"Thank you." Albie glanced at Canon, who nodded. She stepped forward and into Grammie's arms.

Grammie held her, talking softly. Canon couldn't make out the words, but Albie nodded.

Grammie released Albie and stepped back to the dough. "Now kids, let me get these biscuits in the oven, then we can visit your new temporary home." She used a circular cookie cutter, setting the doughy circles on a cookie sheet. Once the pan was in the oven, she washed her hands again. "Canon, put eight minutes on your timer."

"Yes, ma'am." He pulled out his phone and tapped the screen.

"All righty, let's go. Follow me." She pulled open the back door and made an abrupt right turn and pushed the latch of another door. "This unit is the same as mine, but reversed."

"Like our apartments." Albie glanced at Canon, who nodded.

The kitchen was clean, but it felt sterile, with none of the personal touches of a home. It had been updated since his childhood, with Canon making a majority of the cosmetic changes.

Since his book club friend B.J. Johnson worked as a property manager, he had connections for any kind of contractor Canon needed. The flooring man had been recommended by B.J. Canon had worked alongside the floor installer, learning many things.

"I love the floors," Albie declared.

The wood floors had turned out great, and Canon smiled.

"My baby put those in," Grammie Nan proudly stated. "He's handy with tools."

They continued to the living space, which was empty. The walls had been painted pale taupe. A small telephone niche hinted at the age of the building.

The stairwell had an open banister, and the wood steps had white runners. The stairs creaked as they traveled toward the second floor. At the landing, the alarm rang.

"I've got it," Canon said as he turned and headed back downstairs two steps at a time.

Just before he left the apartment, he heard Grammie Nan say, "He's such a good boy and handsome, too. Don't you think?" Canon smiled and saved the biscuits from burning even though his ears were on fire.

He rejoined the women in the larger bedroom. Grammie held sheets in her hand as an air mattress inflated. A thick moss green blanket awaited on a folding metal chair.

As they made the bed, Canon yawned.

"Ah, my poor boy. You are plum tuckered. Let's get some warm food in you, then you can take a shower and nap."

"He's been up all night." Albie said, putting her hands on her hips. "He wouldn't leave me by myself."

"It wasn't the entire night. Just after the fire," Canon yawned again.

"Like you slept well before the fire. That party was

loud."

Grammie led the way to her kitchen. She fixed them plates, and they sat at the small round table overlooking the backyard.

Albie hummed with each bite. She knew how to make Grammie Nan happy. The older woman loved feeding people.

Grammie used to instruct him with little words of wisdom while they ate. She usually chose mealtime because Canon had his mouth full and couldn't reply. He could hear Grammie now. "Food draws people closer. They then agree on what makes them happy. And togetherness is good for the soul. Soul food."

Canon filled his plate twice and tried not to nod off. He covered his mouth and yawned again.

It was nice to be somewhere safe.

Albie's laughter met his ears. He glanced at her. Her dainty hand covered her mouth and nose. Laugh lines edged her eyes. She was staring at him.

He scratched his chest. "What happened?"

"Honey, you fell asleep." Grammie's eyes crinkled too, but she frowned. Concerned, she said, "Up. You need to shower, then off to bed with you."

Canon glanced at the wall clock. "I have a few hours, and then I have to work."

Grammie's eyelids flew open. "No way. You are too tired. Not one of those twenty-four-hour shifts."

"Not this time. Just twelve hours."

Albie gasped.

"I'll be fine. Then I need to go to the apartment and make sure the fire is out." He turned to Albie. "We can see if anything is salvageable."

She nodded and bit her lip. "Mine won't be, but it was all secondhand furniture and clothes are replaceable. Thank God you saved my purse."

Canon stood, scooting his chair back. He picked up his empty plate.

"Leave it be," Grammie ordered.

Albie stood too, and she grabbed him around the waist and hugged him tight. Canon placed a kiss on the top of her head, and she let him go to the other duplex.

Once next door, Canon stumbled up the stairs into the full bath. Twisting on the water, he set the temperature, then disrobed. He hadn't checked to see if there was soap before getting in and was pleased to find a trial size bar and shampoo bottles. The water turned gray as the soot washed down the drain.

Steam filled the bathroom as he reached for the towel hung on the bar. He wiped the mirror, examining the bags under his red eyes. Dang, he needed sleep. In the smaller bedroom, he dropped his dirty clothes in a pile, then with the towel wrapped around his waist, he collapsed onto the air mattress.

CHAPTER SEVEN

ALL EVENING AT THE STATION, Canon's phone blew up. He'd wanted to keep it handy in case Grammie Nan or Albie needed him, but they remained silent. However, all his book club guys had texted or called him, trying to find out what he needed. But when they found out about Albie, they rallied the troops, sending feelers out for clothes, furniture, or anything for a home.

The guys kept inquiring what Albie liked. Canon didn't know much about her, but found himself curious and wanting to get to know her more.

Canon had to wash the trucks. They had one call at two a.m., taking an older gentleman who'd fallen to the hospital. Luckily, he'd not broken anything and only had a slight bump on his head.

After work, around ten that morning, Canon picked up Albie. She'd gone to the store and bought a couple sets of clothes, and now wore a pair of jeans and a cute tailored purple top. They stopped by their apartment building. Albie gaped at the large hole in the wall where her bedroom had been.

"Mister Doodles." With her shoulders slumped, she covered her face.

"I'm sorry, Albie," Canon said, covering her hand with his. "Let's take a look."

Albie inhaled and wiped her face. "Okay."

Canon didn't take the steps two at a time like usual but held Albie's hand as they ascended. The smell of incinerated plastic, burnt wood, and scorched metal hung in the air. The siding had melted, resembling limp spaghetti noodles.

For a moment, they paused, staring at the charred remains of Albie's apartment. She stepped inside, but the floor bowed. On the counter, a lone bowl remained pristine amidst the carnage. "It's my grandma's" She picked it up and cradled it.

The floor creaked and Canon tugged on her arm. "It's not safe."

She clung to Canon, shivering. "If you hadn't come for me…"

"I've got you," he said, pulling her against him and holding her. She exhaled a shuddering breath and clasped her hands behind his back.

"Should we see if your apartment survived?" she asked, stepping away.

Canon held his breath as he pushed open the apartment door. Humidity hung in the air and the carpet squished under his feet. "What a soggy mess. The electronics… Oh man."

He didn't want to think about the money he'd shelled out for that setup. But it was just stuff.

There was standing water on the kitchen floor, and

soot streaked the walls near the ceiling. He opened a cabinet and found the items dusty but salvageable.

Canon continued into his bedroom, pleasantly surprised to see the room intact. The smokey mattress and sheet set would need to be tossed, but the furniture was sound.

He called Brad Davidson. "Hey, I'm at my apartment. My bed and dresser are okay. There are things in the kitchen, like pots and pans too. I'm pretty sure my TV is ruined."

"All right, Canon, I'll get the club and my son-in-law. We'll come get your furniture and whatever else you need." Brad said, "Lunch's on me, too."

"I appreciate your help, but you might have to fight my Grammie on the food. She loves to feed people. She calls it her ministry." Canon laughed.

"We'll see." Brad chuckled. "See you soon."

Something in the other room thumped and Canon jogged into the living room, finding Albie focused on the end table in the corner. The lamp rolled on the floor where it had recently fallen.

"Something is in here," she whispered, keeping her hazel gaze trained on the corner.

A small animal mewed.

Canon bent, staring into the darkness under the table. Golden eyes reflected in the light. "It's a cat. How the heck did a cat get in here?"

"Did you leave your door open the night of the fire?" Albie asked, trying to see past him.

Canon couldn't remember. He thought he had closed his door, but getting out had been his priority and those types of details slipped his mind.

He checked to make sure the door was shut tight now. "If we're going to help the little guy, we can't have him fleeing into the parking lot. I don't want him to get hit by a car. Can you tell if it's Mr. Doodles?"

Albie knelt and strained to see. She gasped and nodded, glancing at Canon with happy tears streaking her face.

Canon found a clean bowl and filled it with water. He sat it down by the corner and stepped back.

"Come on, kitty." Albie coaxed. Eventually the tiny tabby stumbled out with a "mew."

He lapped at the water and revved his motor when Albie stroked his grimy fur. His tail stuck straight in the air. When he'd had his fill, he rubbed on Albie's knee. She picked him up; he batted at her hair.

A knock sounded, and the kitty jumped out of Albie's hands and returned to his hidey-hole.

"Hey," Canon said, opening his door to Jasen and B.J.

"We're here because somebody ordered muscles." B.J. flexed and Jasen laughed.

"That's why I'm with you. I'll work while you talk."

"Before y'all start moving stuff, I need to get Mr. Doodles to the truck," Canon said.

"Doodles? You got a dog?" B.J. asked, glancing around.

Albie moved, catching the men's attention. B.J.

smiled his spider-sizing-up-a-fly grin, and Canon's stomach churned.

"This is my neighbor and friend, Albie. That big black hole over there was her home." Canon pointed across the landing. "We just found her kitten. He's one of the few things that survived the fire."

"We'll help you catch the damn cat," B.J. said, stalking into the room.

"It's okay. He's easy. Watch this." Albie opened the pantry and found a box of pasta.

"When I tell you to shake this box, shake it," she said, thrusting the box at Canon.

She squatted down next to Canon's feet. "Now."

He shook the box of elbow macaroni and the little cat peeked his head out of his cubby. "Come on, kitty," Canon called, "I've got some nice crunchy noodles for you, Mr. Doodles."

The kitten ran over, and Albie scooped him up. "He thinks it's his treats."

Albie cuddled the kitty, and he purred again. She stuck out her hand, palm up, and Canon passed over his keys. She left with the bundle of fur. Canon couldn't help watching the way she practically skipped outside, her happiness bubbling up.

"Ah," B.J. said, "you didn't tell me your neighbor is hot. Maybe she started the fire."

Canon frowned and turned toward B.J. "I didn't know. She wore oversized clothes and always had her hair up. But she is cute."

"Why didn't you shake your love noodle at her?" Jasen teased.

B.J. snickered and nudged his friend. "Good one. Why didn't I think of that?"

Brad, along with daughter Jessie and son-in-law Josiah, crowded the doorway. "The gang is all here," Brad announced.

"Not quite. We're missing the Greene ginger and the sexual deviant." B.J. laughed.

"Greene ginger present." Forrest squeezed past Brad and into the room. "RIP flat screen. You will be missed, but only until you're replaced."

"The sexual deviant has plans with his wife today," Brad said. "I'm pretty sure Parker would like that nickname."

"At least Lisa would," Jessie added with a giggle.

"I've got my SUV, Josiah brought his truck, and I saw B.J.'s too, so we've got enough vehicles to move your furniture."

"I brought my extra totes," Jessie said.

"Really?" Canon breathed. "I can't believe it."

"They're just storage totes, Canon." Jessie cocked her head to the side, putting her hands on her hips.

"But they're for romance books. Your grandma's book stash. The original dare." Canon picked up a tote with a wide smile.

"Good ol' Armando." B.J. declared as he winked at Jessie.

"Who's Armando?" Albie asked from the doorway.

"A sexy hero from a book," Jessie said, sticking her hand out for Albie. The women shook. "I'm Jessie Barnes. This is my husband, Josiah, and my daddy, Brad." The men waved.

"Do you like romance?" B.J. asked Albie.

Her cheeks flared red. "I, uh—" She glanced at Canon.

"Jessie lives in the house where the romance novel fad started. Her grandma collected the books." Canon came to stand next to Albie.

"She hoarded the damn things," B.J. added. "But Jessie dared me to read a few, and then I dared others. And, voilà, we have our book club."

"Speaking of dares…" Forrest's gaze slid from Canon to Albie.

"Not today," Canon groaned, rubbing his face.

"Canon is right. Let's load up his stuff." Brad said, coming to his rescue.

Jessie and Albie sorted the kitchen items and Forrest and B.J. carried out the full totes. Jasen orchestrated the move like a conductor. They emptied Canon's dresser and nightstand into the totes then hoisted them to the trucks. They propped the mattress against the wall and removed the bed slats.

Jessie and Albie moved to the bathroom and emptied the medicine cabinet and the cabinet under the sink. "I think your storage space is bigger than mine," Albie said to Canon as he passed in the hallway.

"Probably not," Jasen said, sticking his head in the

room. "Canon is a neat freak."

"Just a little," Canon admitted, holding part of the headboard. He lowered the board and wiped his hands on his jeans.

"I have something for you, Albie," Jessie said.

"What's that?" Albie said softly.

"I called Canon's grandma and had her spy, so I had the right size. I brought you a bra and panty set." Jessie owned Double D Intimates, a high-end lingerie business that made each piece by hand.

"Thank you," Albie said, sounding emotional.

"Let's take a break, and I'll show you." Jessie stepped out and almost squashed Canon's foot with her cowgirl boot. "Oops," she said, tilting her head and zeroing on his crimson face.

"Come on, Canon," Josiah barked. "Let's get this out of the way." He kissed Jessie on the cheek, then lifted his end. Canon led the way down the stairs, and they loaded it onto Josiah's truck.

Jessie and Albie followed them. When Canon met Albie's gaze, she quickly glanced away with a deep blush. His stomach fluttered, and he clutched it.

Josiah slapped a hand on Canon's shoulder. "Be patient. She'll come around."

Canon started, "But I didn't say—"

"Everyone can tell," Josiah said with a wink.

"Tell what?"

"She's totally into you." Josiah walked away.

Canon stayed outside, digesting what Josiah had

revealed. Could it be true? Heat pooled, and he longed to find out.

CHAPTER EIGHT

A FEW DAYS LATER, CANON walked into the duplex he and Albie were still sharing. It was quiet. Albie's car was out front, but besides Mr. Doodle, nothing moved. The cat, at least, had peered up from his warm spot in a sunbeam.

He heard laughter next door. Grammie Nan was having her weekly tea. She was rather famous for her sweet tea. The ladies would flock to Grammie's house, taking turns bringing scrumptious goodies.

He always looked forward to visiting with them when he had the chance. Grammie would show him off, and he would get to sample everything. Today, he wasn't as eager to visit. He had wanted to chill and hang out with Albie.

He'd learned that she worked for an accountant and was the liaison for Stitt's Truck Stop, among other Fortuna businesses. He would have never guessed by the way she'd dressed. But she had informed him that's the way she dresses for the gym.

Canon changed and bounded down the stairs and out the front door. One more glance up and down the street before he pulled open the door to Grammie Nan's house.

"There's my boy. Isn't he handsome?" Grammie said.

Grammie's friends cooed and a short old lady named Desire Hardmann pinched his butt as he walked by. He was glad it was his backside this time.

"Hi, Grammie," He reached for her and pulled her to her feet. Then he hugged her, lifting her. All her friends gasped, giggled, and exclaimed like they always did.

"Put me down," Grammie huffed with pink cheeks and a smile. "You'll break me in two." This time, she tapped his crown with a romance novel. Once he set her on her feet, Canon snatched the book from her hand.

"Oh, this is good," he said. "It has an unpredictable ending."

"I beg to differ. It's predictable," Desire stated. "It's a romance. They all end with happy ever after."

"Yeah," Canon agreed, stepping out of her reach. "Isn't that cool? Love triumphs all."

"Even fires?" He twisted to see Albie sitting between two of Grammie's regulars. A pretty blush deepened as she lifted her cup to her lips. He stood mesmerized as she sipped.

"Sometimes it's the love that sets the fire," Desire said, wiggling her brows.

Canon smirked, feeling his face heat. "I'll just get a glass of tea and see myself out."

"Get some of my sticky buns," Desire said, waggling her eyebrows again.

When Albie returned from the tea, she headed upstairs. From his place on his bed, he saw her top the landing. He laid stretched out in his basketball shorts and no shirt, reading a book, one hand behind his head to prop him on the pillow. She glanced at him, squeaked, and hurried into her room.

He sat up, curling his toes in the carpet. His new mattress was comfortable, but the softness did nothing for the butterflies in his stomach.

He and Albie had become roommates and friends. Sharing TV time and caring for Mr. Doodles. One night while watching TV, she fell asleep with her head on his lap. They'd shopped to get her a secondhand bedroom set. Together, they had painted it. And every time she hugged him, she held on longer than a usual hug until he kissed her head.

Canon's phone chimed, pulling him out of his daydream. "Man up and ask her out," Brad texted. The older man hadn't teased him about Albie, especially after Canon had opened up after book club.

"To what?" Canon volleyed.

"Dinner. A movie. A moonlit walk. I don't know your girl, you do. You choose."

Canon smiled and warmth filled him. *His girl.*

Brad texted again. "The Dare."

Canon swallowed and opened a book to where he'd hidden his dare papers. A superhero, a train set in the past. He folded them and squared his shoulders. "AImee, wish me luck."

"Good luck, Canon," his new home AI responded.

He tapped on Albie's door. "Come in."

"Hey, I uh—" Canon's mouth went dry.

"What do you think?" she asked, swirling. The red dress skirt flared as she spun. Her toned legs caught his attention. He swallowed and motioned for her to spin again.

"Nice."

"Do you think so?"

"What's it for?"

She tilted her head as if debating to tell him. "Well, I was hoping—"

Ring! The doorbell clanged. "I'll get it." Before he left, he winked, and she blushed.

He took the steps three at a time, hoping whoever it was would be quick. Canon opened the door and found a smirking B.J., holding a handful of novels.

"Hello, I was talking to Brad about you-know-what." B.J.'s gaze shifted as he leaned left, peering over Canon's shoulder. "We found these in the book hoard. Thought they might give you some ideas you can research." He wiggled his brows.

Canon sighed. Behind him, the stairs creaked, and he hoped Albie had changed.

"Are you going to invite me in?" B.J. asked, stepping into the room. "Hello, Albie. You look like a dream come true."

"Thank you." Albie glanced from one man to the other. "How will reading romance novels be research?" she asked, one dainty brow raised.

"Oh boy," Canon mumbled, rubbing the back of his head. "Thanks a lot," he growled to B.J.

Ignoring Canon, B.J. stepped closer toward the stairs. "I'd be happy to enlighten you. Would you care to join me for a drink?"

Canon clenched his fists as heat rose to his face.

Albie skipped down the stairs to Canon's side. She slipped her arm through his and placed her head on his shoulder. "That's very kind of you, B.J., but Canon and I have plans."

Instantly, the anger that had been building slipped away. He smiled down at her.

B.J. rocked back on his boots and snapped his hand. "That's a shame. I hear there's a great deal on dinner at Hammered tonight."

"Would you like to get dinner?" Canon asked Albie. A new warmth spread in his gut.

"That sounds perfect." She tiptoed and kissed his cheek. "Thanks for asking. I'll finish getting ready."

"Wait—" B.J. said, stopping her in her tracks. "You look great already. What more is there?"

She blushed and glanced down at her feet.

Canon offered, "Her jewelry. And she likes to put this thickener stuff on her lashes. It really makes them pop, although they're spectacular without them."

"You are an observant one," B.J. teased with a laugh.

"He's my hero," Albie said, reaching the steps.

"That's perfect! It fits the dare perfectly." B.J. slapped Canon on the back.

Albie's eyes narrowed, and she stopped three steps up. "What dare?"

The happy warmth dissipated, and Canon's stomach turned to lead. "I will explain at dinner. B.J., the king of dares, is something else."

CHAPTER NINE

CANON TUGGED ON HIS POLO shirt collar as he nursed a long-neck beer while Albie sipped her sweet tea. As they waited for their food, Canon spotted Parker and Lisa reading together in Hammered's corner booth. B.J. and Jasen sat at the bar and kept checking on him while Forrest, along with his wife and daughter, ate at another table. Only Brad and Ophelia were missing.

"The dare?" Albie asked.

The door opened and, low and behold, Brad and Ophelia waltzed inside. They paused at a bookshelf filled with romance books. Brad met Canon's gaze and tipped his cowboy hat.

Every one of his book club members had arrived. *Was this a conspiracy?*

Albie cleared her throat, capturing Canon's attention again. He leaned forward. "We read romance novels. Brad, B.J., Forrest, Parker, Jasen, Ophelia, and I. We don't read the same book each week. We pick a genre or a trope. Once we did a location: Texas. When we're finished, we switch books. Ophelia is the town librarian, and she moderates the group." He waved toward the librarian. She grinned and waved back. "Oh, if you need to find a good book, just ask Ophelia. She'll hook you up."

"And the dare," Albie insisted, glancing at Ophelia.

"The book club went camping. It was awesome. There was an enormous bonfire and Parker made his award-winning chili." Canon closed his eyes and hummed. Albie giggled and his lids popped open again. "Anyway, the point of the camping trip was to pick the next type of book to read."

Albie fingered the plastic soda glass. He swallowed at the intensity of her stare. "After dinner, B.J. got all worked up and asked us each to think of a character, genre, and setting and write them on separate pieces of paper. The character was very general, like a bartender or clown. The genre could also be a trope like secret baby or, my favorite, friends to lovers."

Canon sipped his beer.

"So, the setting is speculative, too? Like Times Square or Mars?" Albie asked.

"Yes. All vague, like Australia or a diner." Canon glanced toward the bar. B.J. and Jasen nudged each other. "Then B.J. had us draw from a hat."

She leaned forward with wide eyes and asked, "What is the club reading?"

"Sci-fi, but that's not what the hat was about. We each drew a character, genre, and setting, then B.J. dared us to act it out with a significant other."

"Oh." Albie straightened and glanced over at the other men. "B.J. is a strange cat."

Canon chuckled and relaxed against the booth. "You

can say that again."

"B.J. is a strange cat," she giggled with her eyes crinkled in mirth.

Heat flashed over Canon, and his heart rate spiked. He loved the way she laughed.

"What did he dare you to do?" Albie asked through fluttering lashes, then she glanced at her plate. "Or have you already done it?"

His heart stalled, and he leaned forward again. "I haven't. I picked superhero, historical, and a train. And I haven't worked out the dare yet. Besides Grammie Nan and Ophelia, you're the only other lady I'm around a lot."

A pretty blush crept onto Albie's cheeks. "What do you have to do to fulfill the dare?"

Canon crossed his arms. "Have you heard about *The Visitation*?"

Albie clasped her hands together on the table. "You mean that angel story?"

"In Fortuna, that story is cherished. Not only do couples read it together, but the men dress in angel wings and visit their sweethearts while they sleep." With a quick nod in Parker's direction, he continued, "And some try things in public and get caught by the police."

The Fords flipped a page in the book they read. Lisa turned red and buried her face in Parker's neck. He smiled and patted his wife's hands. "It's amazing to me what romance novels have done for the Fords. They were on the brink of divorce, arguing in public. Then B.J. dared him to read a romance. He acted out favorite heroes for his wife, and now she's the envy of Fortuna."

"What did he receive at the camp out?" Albie asked, studying the couple.

"Scotland and a billionaire with a hidden past." Canon stared at the ceiling. "That's all I can remember."

Albie scooted forward with her elbows on the table and chin in her hands. "Are you going to wear tights?"

"What color do you think?" Canon asked with a smirk. Albie giggled. He continued. "Brad actually suggested I could skip the whole modern hero suit by going old school with the Lone Ranger."

She blinked with a dreamy expression. "I can see you in a mask and cowboy hat."

He mimicked her with his elbows on the table, chin in hands. "You can, huh?"

"Although, I think going with an already established hero is cliché. You should invent a new one."

He sat back again. His mind whirled. Could he invent a hero Albie would approve of? He glanced toward the book club members. Jasen winked and B.J. gave him a thumbs up. Canon rubbed his face, and a grin broke out. A little superhero brainstorming session was in order.

CHAPTER TEN

CANON SHIFTED HIS WEIGHT, GLANCING down the street to the sidewalk food vendor's cart. The longer he waited for his friends to join him at the party store, the hungrier he became. He stuffed his hands in his front pockets and turned his back on the sight. The smell of pan fried burgers and sausages continued to taunt him.

"Hey, Canon," Jasen hollered, hurrying toward him with a giant sausage loaded with sauerkraut in his hand. He brought it to his lips and took a large bite.

"Ah man, you're killing me. That smells heavenly." Canon clutched his stomach as Jasen took another bite.

Jasen closed his eyes and chewed. He swallowed. "I have to scarf it down fast. I've only got so much time on my lunch break."

"Sure, I get it. I don't have to like it, though." Canon grinned. His stomach rumbled loudly in agreement, and they laughed.

"I'm here. The party can start," B.J. announced, sauntering up.

Jasen opened his mouth to answer, but a horn honked as a yellow convertible pulled into an empty spot across the street. It was the kind of little car a teenaged girl would drive and something Grammie would love. Parker hefted his girth out of the bucket seat. Every time Canon saw him, Parker drove an unfamiliar car. Such was the nature of being a used car dealer.

"Howdy," Parker greeted with a wave.

"I thought you might be a hot chick in the banana car," B.J. said, tipping his mirrored shades down.

"I just got it and wanted to see if anything was wrong with it." Parker glanced at the car. "I don't want it to turn out to be a lemon."

"It's the right color for it," Canon teased.

"Speaking of color, what superhero look are you going for?" Jasen asked.

"Superheroes usually wear primary colors," Parker suggested.

"Not the Hulk or Green Lantern," B.J. pointed out.

"Or Batman." Jasen added.

"Okay, you're right. Some don't wear primary but most wear yellow, red, and blue." Parker put a finger in the air, "Or some combination of those. Like Superman, Spider-Man, or Iron Man."

"All the cool *mans* have bright colors," B.J. said.

"Not Batman." Jasen countered.

"I said all the cool ones." B.J. smirked and placed his hands on his hips.

Jasen frowned. "Batman is the coolest."

"No way. He doesn't even have a superpower." B.J. shot back.

"That's what makes him awesome," Jasen

proclaimed. "He's the average Joe."

"Not really. He's got a bah-zillion dollars," Canon stated.

"I know what to get you punks for Christmas." Parker aimed his remark at Jasen and B.J. "Iron Man and Batman jammies."

"Oh, good." Brad joined them, shaking Canon's hand. "I see the circus is in town. You're hanging out with the clowns."

Canon laughed. His phone vibrated. "Forrest is coming. He said to go on in, and he'll meet us there."

Brad pulled open the door and held it as the guys filtered in. The employees knew they were in the Fortuna Dare Society book club and whispered as they passed. Canon flashed hot and hurried toward the room with the costumes.

They shuffled through the items on the rack. "How about Mr. Incredible?" B.J. asked.

"Nice puffy muscles," Jasen laughed.

"Canon doesn't need them, but you two do," Brad teased, earning raised brows from the group.

"Thanks," Canon nodded at Brad. Sometimes Jasen and B.J. could be hard to handle, and Canon appreciated the older man coming to his aid and wrangling their attention.

"See primary colors," Parker motioned to the rack.

After sifting through the various racks, Canon concluded. "I think I need to invent my own."

"No Lone Ranger?" Brad asked.

"Any ideas?" Parker studied Canon.

"No, that's why I wanted your help," Canon admitted with a shrug.

"Okay, let's brainstorm. Canon is young, he works at the firehouse and is an EMT," Jasen mused, rubbing his scruff.

"EMT man?" B.J. laughed.

"What about Fire Man?" Forrest quipped, walking into the room.

"Fire Man." Canon rolled the words around.

"That's brilliant!" Jasen laughed.

"Thank you," Forrest said with a flourish and a bow.

"I like it." Canon clapped his hands together. "Now for the costume."

The men stood staring at the shelves and costumes. "He doesn't need a full costume. Maybe just a mask?" Brad picked up a plastic mask that only covered the eyes.

"Wait, what kind of superpowers does Fire Man have?" Jasen asked.

"Putting out fires?" Forrest suggested.

"No, too cliché." Canon shook his head.

"Or he can start fires. There's kind of no in between." Forrest shifted more costumes to the right.

"Unless he's Full-of-Smoke-Man," Parker laughed.

"Maybe he should fart fire," Forrest muttered, trying to bite back a laugh.

Canon winced. "Why would I do that on a date with someone I actually want to impress?"

"A better question is: how could you *flart* without

singeing your butt hairs?" B.J. threw out.

The group cringed.

"Fart Man isn't happening, so nothing more about it. And I'm not breathing fire either." Canon scowled at B.J.

"You'd have to have dragon breath," Brad shrugged.

Canon covered his face and shook his head. *Maybe brainstorming with the book club was a bad idea.*

"Just snap your fingers and have a flame appear. It's magic. I'm sure you can figure it out if you search online." Jasen tapped his chin.

Canon nodded. "I like that."

Forrest offered Canon a red tube. "What if, instead of a wig or mask, you color your hair? This stuff will wash out and doesn't smell funky."

Canon took and uncapped it. Forrest was right. It hardly smelled.

"You cannot recreate the ginger, but you can try." Forrest ran his fingers through his hair, then stroked his beard.

"Actually," Jasen said, picking up a yellow tube, "How about using this too? Spike the top, then use the red on the tips."

"Or the red first with yellow tips," Brad suggested.

"Use both. I got it." Canon took both tubes. "What should I wear?"

"Red leggings," Parker said, trying not to laugh.

B.J. snickered. "Just a T-shirt with an F on it."

"Fart Man," Jasen blurted, elbowing B.J.

Brad rolled his eyes. "Go to the thrift store and find a

shirt. You can paint or draw an F in a circle or whatever."

Canon nodded and picked up an orange oval shaped mask. He could slip it over his head easily enough. "Thanks guys."

"I need to get back to work," Jasen said. "Thanks for the distraction."

"Your taxpayer dollars at work," B.J. teased.

"That's right," Jasen winked, then exited.

Canon made the purchase. As he left, both Parker and Forrest, the married men, waited to be rung up. Canon had shifted his eyes elsewhere but hadn't been fast enough to unsee what the men were happily purchasing.

The gift shop had recently received a new shipment of body paint. He couldn't unsee the glee in Parker's eyes, but maybe a foot-long wiener from Hamish's Burger Wagon would distract him. His stomach grumbled in agreement.

CHAPTER ELEVEN

Canon squeezed yellow hair paint into his hand and finger combed his hair. He tried several times to perfect the coloring and thought he had the best look. He rubbed it to the root, then he squirted a dab of red and selected a few hairs as red peaks. The effect was cool.

"Oh," he frowned. He should have put the T-shirt on first.

A knock on the bathroom door startled him. "Almost done?" Albie asked in a soft voice.

"Um, don't open the door," he frantically cleaned up his mess. "You can't see me."

"I know. There's a door in the way," Albie giggled.

"Give me a few minutes and the bathroom is yours."

"Okay," she sighed. "I can't wait to see your costume."

After carefully pulling the shirt over his head, he opened the bathroom door and peeked out, making sure Albie wasn't watching. He didn't want her ruining the surprise. He hurried to his bedroom and shut the door, then hollered, "I'm out."

"Finally," she said in a teasing, singsong voice. "You took longer than my preteen sister."

Canon dressed, then grabbed his mask. He studied the image in the mirror, lifting the orange mask to cover his eyes.

"Done. I'll meet you downstairs," Albie called as she walked by. The stairs creaked as she descended.

Butterflies took flight in his gut. Could he pass as a hero, or would Albie think he was a douche? So far, she'd been a good sport about the dare. Finally, tying the laces on his high-tops, he summoned his courage and leaned over the banister.

Albie sat on the sofa in that short, sexy red dress. She stretched out her shapely legs and crossed her ankles. Mr. Doodles curled next to her. The kitten's ears rotated toward him, and Albie glanced up. Her eyes crinkled, and a hand flew to her mouth.

Canon sucked in a deep breath, puffed out his chest, and strutted down the stairs.

She giggled as her gaze raked him from head to toe, then back up again. Canon must really be Fire Man because heat pooled in his torso and if he farted, he'd probably burn the house down. He would never admit it to B.J., though.

"Oh, my God. Let's see. Red Converse with realistic-looking fire socks. Those are cool. Red basketball shorts, shirt with an F ringed in flames. Again, very cool. I love your hair." She stepped toward him and reached out to touch it, but thought better of it and lowered her hand again. She gasped. "Your eyes!"

Canon smirked and leaned in, staring into her hazel

gaze.

"I love it! They are so freaky. It looks like there's fire in your eyes," she clapped.

"They're contacts. Don't let me rub my eyes or I might lose one."

Albie nodded. She tapped her chin, studying the F on his chest. "I have a date with a superhero. Which one? F for Flame Man?"

Canon shook his head.

"Flame Resistant? Flame Broiled? or Flame Retardant?" she guessed.

"Don't even say the word retardant to B.J. He would have a field day with that one." Canon doubled over, laughing. When he sobered, he asked, "Do you give up?"

She nodded. "Tell me. Who are you?"

Canon squared, then thrust his shoulders out, striking a pose with his hands on his hips. "My fair lady, you have given many heartfelt attempts, but you have failed to identify me correctly. Since I am unnamed, I will keep my identity hidden until such time as my powers are needed."

"You aren't going to tell me?" Albie jutted out her bottom lip, leaned against him, and traced the F on his chest. Her fingertip tickled and scorched as it slid over his skin. Fire was Albie's superpower, not his.

"I'm sorry," He bonked her nose and moved toward the door.

She placed her hands on his hips. "I'll figure it out."

"I hope so."

Canon had made a reservation at the Pink Taco Mexican restaurant. The patrons stared at them as they followed the owner, Clint Torres, to the back-most table. Canon wasn't the only one in costume. Clint wore a mariachi uniform matching the bands. They ordered food and the margarita special of the night.

A mariachi band meandered through the room playing songs. They stopped near Canon's table, then handed Albie a red rose when the love song was over. Then a man arrived and made homemade guacamole and salsa at the table.

"Bless my soul," Desire Hardmann said as she appeared next to Albie. "I didn't believe it. When I got the text, I had to run right over."

Desire appeared fresh from bible study with her pink skirt suit and gray pearl button shirt, but Canon doubted she'd been there with that devilish grin on her face.

"What text?" Albie asked.

"The whole town knows about the book club dare. And your date," Desire thumbed over her shoulder at the other patrons.

Canon and Albie glanced around the restaurant. Every seat had filled. Pairs of eyes gazed at them, blinking.

"Everyone loves a good romance," Canon whispered in shock.

"Tonight it's ours," Albie said, then quickly glanced at the napkin in her lap.

"Honey, can I join you?" Desire asked Albie.

Albie's head snapped up. She shook it, her long hair

flaring out.

Desire cackled like a witch. "I don't blame you one bit. Your Fire Man is sizzling. I'd love for him to cook his bacon on my stove." She fanned herself. Not one hair on her Vulcan-like do moved.

"I'm sorry, Miss Hardmann. Albie's my only special lady tonight," Canon said, turning on an alluring smile.

"Ah, that's a shame," Desire pouted her glossy lips. She nudged Albie's shoulder and said loudly, "If I were you, I'd let your Fire Man use his magic hose on you." She wiggled her eyebrows, then cackled again.

In unison, the restaurant burst into laughter. Desire departed and joined another table.

"Do you have a magic hose, *Fire Man*?" Albie asked, blushing the same shade of red as her dress.

"You got it! Nice." Canon's eyes widened. "Oh, I mean about the name."

She giggled.

"Look." Canon raised his hand, drawing her gaze. He snapped his fingers and a small flame appeared.

"Wow! Fire Man, you are pretty hot."

Canon's face felt as hot as when he ate the spicy salsa. He snapped again, extinguishing the flame.

"How'd you do that?" She canted her head, her inquisitive gaze focused on his hand.

"I can't—"

"A magician doesn't reveal his tricks," she said, crossing her arms and leaning backward.

Canon shook his head. "It's not that. I'm not a

magician or I'd be happy to tell you, but I'm a hero. I was born this way."

"What way?"

"Hot."

Albie rolled her eyes and laughed.

The food arrived, and the band returned and played. Albie trickled the hot sauce on her burrito.

"Not spicy enough for you?" Clint asked.

Albie glanced up at him with round, seemingly innocent, eyes. "I like my food like my man—hot."

"Yes, ma'am." Clint cracked a grin as he refilled her water glass. "Just make sure your meal is scrumptious like your man." He winked at Canon, then disappeared.

Canon couldn't remove the smirk that had found residence on his lips. He met Brad's gaze as the rancher sat at the bar next to the mayor. He raised a bottle of cerveza and saluted.

Canon's phone vibrated, and he glimpsed B.J.'s text: you need a train, don't forget.

Canon tapped the camera and snapped a photo of the mural next to him. On the mountainside, a steam engine chugged down a track. He sent the photo to the group chat.

B.J. texted the poop emoji.

Then Jasen typed the wind emoji and wrote "man." Canon shook his head and glanced over at Jasen. Although Flart Man might be a thing after the refried beans he had consumed.

"Are you too stuffed for dessert?" he asked.

"Not if you share it with me." She blushed and scooted over, tapping the seat next to her.

"Are you sure you want me to come closer? My fiery eyes are creepy," he reminded.

"She wants to play with your hose," Desire said as she passed on her way toward the bathroom.

Albie giggled, burying her face in her hands. "Oh my God, that lady. She's so dirty."

"Yes, and she entertains the whole town. She's a Fortuna treasure." Canon slipped in beside Albie and patted her petite hand.

"I'm not sure if treasure is the right word, but priceless fits."

Clint brought out fried ice cream and two spoons. Against Albie, their shoulders and thighs touching, Canon's heart worked overtime. Under the table she threaded fingers with his, then smiled shyly.

Canon idly imagined steam rising from his head as his hair burned like Moses' bush. Love was magic and everyone loves a good romance.

Hand in hand, they walked toward the fountain in the center of the park. The calming sound of the sprinkling water was the backdrop as they stopped and faced each other. He stared down into her eyes, and she bit her lip, then giggled.

"I'm sorry," she whispered. "It's those contacts. It's hard to be serious wi—"

Canon bent in and claimed her lips. She squeaked, then sighed against him. His heart hammered, and he touched her cheek. He pulled back. "I've been wanting to do that all night."

"You have?" she asked breathlessly.

Canon frowned. "Yes. Before tonight even."

Her brow dipped. "Why the hell haven't you?"

"I d—"

This time, she clenched his shirt and pulled him to her. Her tongue licked the seam of his lips and he opened for her. He moaned and clutched her shoulders, thinking he was off center and would tip over. When they ended the kiss, he placed his forehead on hers and sighed.

Murmurs met his ears. "Please tell me we don't have an audience," he whispered.

"The good news is that only half the restaurant is watching us."

"Is there bad news?"

"The bad news is that half the restaurant is watching us."

He laughed, then said, "Let them watch." He tipped her chin, and she grabbed his biceps as he placed a toe curling kiss on her lips once more. Toward the end, with his hands on her back, he dipped her. When she stood upright, she seemed dazed. He took her hand and lifted it, then swirled her. Her dress flared.

"Best date ever," Albie said, grinning up at him.

"I made an impression."

"Just a little."

"It will get bigger if you touch it," a woman's voice called from somewhere. Canon recognized it as Desire's.

Canon groaned and turned around with hands on his hips. "Seriously?" Canon yelled to the crowd. "Go read your own dang novels and quit being voyeurs."

B.J. uttered something about college words, then Canon spied him and Jasen walking away.

"So, the magic hose grows when you touch it?" Albie asked with a giggle.

He scrubbed his face. "It doesn't need to be touched. Sometimes it just grows." He shrugged.

"Like magic." Albie's smile widened.

Desire's witch-like laughter echoed through the night.

CHAPTER TWELVE

When Canon awoke, Albie wasn't there. He glanced at the time and grumbled, "It's late." He reached for the light and sat up.

His pillowcase was streaked red, orange, and yellow. He rubbed his face and when he pulled his hands away, they were discolored and sticky. He groaned.

Canon strode to the shower and scrubbed his hair until the water ran clear. Sighing, he remembered Albie's body snuggled against his. Suddenly, his manhood sprang to life. Maybe they could have another round before he left for work.

He wrapped the towel around his waist and headed to Albie's bedroom. "Albie?" he rapped on the door with his knuckles. Her bed was pristine, but he reminded himself that she hadn't slept in it.

After the public kiss, they hadn't been able to keep their hands off each other. They'd made it home and fell into bed.

"Wow." Canon envisioned her curves pressed against him. He moseyed into the kitchen for a bowl of cereal. Mr. Doodles' bowl was empty. He took the cat food and shook it. Usually, the fur ball came running, but this time silence met his ears.

"Here kitty," Canon called, searching the first floor. Not finding the kitten, he bounded upstairs.

He paused in the bathroom. Albie's makeup wasn't on the counter. His heart dropped. He threw back the shower curtain. No shampoo or conditioner. No pink scrubby thing.

Canon held his breath as he hurried into her room. Her closet was ajar. Opening it, he found empty hangers.

He tried to keep the panic at bay as he scurried through the duplex, hunting for a note. When he looked outside for her car, it wasn't there.

"What went wrong?" Canon sunk onto the sofa with his elbows on his knees. He covered his face.

"We made love, then she fell asleep in my arms." Goosebumps appeared on his flesh as he remembered her lips on his neck trailing down to his chest. She hadn't reacted negatively to his touch.

"Why has she gone?" His gut churned, and his shoulders hunched with the weight of rejection. "Why did she take the flipping cat?" Of course, Mr. Doodles was hers.

Canon needed to workout. He changed his clothes and packed a bag. He had a forty-eight-hour shift starting soon. As he exited the apartment, Grammie Nan called from her door, "Canon, where's the fire?"

He stopped but couldn't face her. He heaved a sigh and hoped she'd let him alone. "Hitting the gym, Grammie."

"Honey, what's wrong?" Her sympathetic tone made his breath hitch. The porch floor creaked as she stepped near.

He sighed. Canon knew better than to gloss over his feelings. His head drooped. "Albie left."

"I know. She told me she was going," Grammie Nan informed, approaching him.

Canon lifted his head and met her gaze. "She did? How come she didn't tell me?" A bolt of betrayal zapped his heart.

"Come here, baby doll." Grammie opened her arms, and he fell into them. She patted his back. "I don't know why she didn't tell you, but I saw her hurry out this morning. She was smiling, and that's saying something after catching a cat to put in the pet carrier. I'll get you some cookies."

Canon nodded and gently squeezed her. "Thanks, Grammie. You always know how to make me feel better."

At the station house, he threw his bag on the bench and stretched. He started on the treadmill, putting his earbuds in so he didn't have to look at his phone.

Notifications kept chiming, but he chose to ignore them. It was the book club guys. Forrest had seen him driving and tried to be friendly. Canon's greeting must not have appeared genuine. Now they were vying for information about his date. He'd love to commiserate but didn't think his raw emotions could take more prodding.

The day dragged on.

The next morning, when he looked at his phone, he saw he had a voicemail dated early the previous day. His heart leaped as he recognized Albie's number.

He played the recorded message. She mumbled to the cat as she shuffled around. The car door opened, the car chimed, the cat meowed, and then the words tumbled out. "I meant to tell you sooner, but I thought we'd have more time." She paused and sighed. "I'm sorry to leave—" the connection cut out and garbled her words. "No way to—" then the call ended.

Canon's hope was stomped on and chucked into the pit of despair along with his heart. "So much for being a B'SHOAF."

At the end of his shift, B.J. waited, arms crossed, leaning against the post on Canon's porch. The deep scowl on B.J.'s face was etched as if he had been loitering for days.

They didn't speak, and B.J. followed Canon inside like a stray cat. Canon strode to the kitchen and opened the fridge, going for a beer. He lifted a bottle to his guest. B.J. nodded, took the longneck and pulled out a chair at the small table. He didn't speak, and it was both reassuring and alarming.

After half the beer, B.J. finally spoke. "I finished the next book. It was pretty good, and it only took me two evenings. Thought you'd want the distraction."

Canon tipped back and examined him. "How did you know?"

B.J. shrugged. "I have excellent detective skills."

When his attempt at humor fell flat, he said, "At first, since you weren't spilling any beans about your date, we thought you got lucky."

Canon's face heated, and he crossed his arms.

"Then when you kept ignoring us, we thought you were mad about the restaurant. The longer the silence lasted, the more anxious Jasen became. He's a worrywart and sent me to—"

"Sate his curiosity," Canon mumbled.

"Check on you. Hell, I was worried, too. We are all worried."

Canon stared at the clock on the microwave, waiting for the minute to change.

"Then I talked with Nan," B.J. admitted.

Canon's gaze slid to meet B.J.'s. "And?"

"And she told me about Albie leaving." B.J. lifted his bottle.

Canon squeezed his eyes shut and rubbed them. A sigh escaped. "I don't know what I did wrong."

B.J. slapped his back. "Don't worry about it. Chicks are weird." He glanced at his watch, then stood and tossed the empty bottle into the recycling bin. "Jasen should be here any time with pizza. I think Brad is bringing Chinese, and Forrest is grabbing a movie."

"Parker?" Canon asked. He rubbed his chest, feeling the weight subside some.

"Beer."

Canon sighed again. Tears welled, but he blinked them away.

"It's okay, asshole, I cry for beer too," B.J. winked.

Canon laughed until he doubled over. God, he needed his friends. His book club.

The doorbell rang. Canon let Jasen in.

"The za is here," Jasen sung. The smell of pizza filled the room.

Soon Brad and Parker arrived. Luckily, Brad thought about bringing paper plates because Canon didn't have enough clean dishes.

"When's the gingerbread man going to get here?" B.J. grumbled.

"Go ahead and eat," Brad said, thrusting a paper plate in his face.

Canon opened a roll of paper towels and brought it to the living room. He glanced around the space. The sofa would accommodate three men, but other than the coffee table and TV console, he didn't have any furniture. He turned to Jasen. "Grab a chair from the kitchen. We'll need three. Be right back."

Canon visited Grammie Nan and borrowed her TV trays. When he returned, Forrest had arrived. He was shoveling lo mien noodles into his mouth with his eyes rolling back in his head.

"Oh, this is heaven. I haven't had Chinese in so long. Ever since Ivy was pregnant, Chinese food makes her wheezy. We haven't had it." Forrest moaned again.

"Get a room," Parker teased.

"I'm in one," Forrest countered.

On the coffee table were three movie cases. Deadpool,

Star Wars: A New Hope, and The Godfather. "What should we watch?" Jasen glanced at Canon, who shrugged. "Star Wars?"

B.J. opened the case. He held up the DVD. "What the hell, Forrest?"

"I didn't put that in there. Ivy must have put it in the wrong case."

"I am not watching Jar Jar Binks. I'd rather stick forks in my eyes and electrocute my testicles," B.J. uttered, leaning forward and crossing his arms.

"Okay, The Godfather?" Brad suggested.

B.J. again opened the case and laughed. "Paw Patrol. Try again."

"That leaves Deadpool." Parker took a seat on the sofa with a plate of pizza.

"I'm afraid to look at it." B.J. opened the player and set the disc in without checking it. "We get what we get."

The men set their books on the table and talked over the plot similarities. "You'll like the cat star book."

Forrest leaned forward. "Oh, did the alien have a magic wanker?"

"Actually, no." B.J. turned red. "It was magical semen."

"They are part of the navel academy?" Brad asked.

"Ha. Ha. No. Alien jizz reacted biochemically to the females' bodies, making them physiologically have the best orgasms of their lives. Other species can't compete."

"Dude, that's some conflict for you," Jasen said, rubbing his eyes.

"I know, right?" B.J. said, "The magic-spunk aliens are used in the sex industry and the ladies line up, but the males never find love. And their species is being hunted to extinction."

Canon stared at the muted TV as the third kids' movie trailer rolled by. "Is it me, or are there a lot of kids' previews for a Deadpool movie? It doesn't seem right."

"Uh oh," Forrest muttered.

"What is it?" Brad asked as the Disney castle appeared.

"Oh shit. Whatever cartoon crap this is, I will still watch it over Jar Jar Binks." B.J. declared, glancing around for a consensus.

"You just don't want to electrocute your testicles," Brad said with a chuckle.

"You mean electro-ugly," Jasen teased.

The title Frozen appeared on the screen. "Oh shit," B.J. repeated.

"Anyone ever seen it?" Forrest asked. They shook their heads or replied negatively. "It's a musical, and it's actually not bad. Decent plot and all that."

The men sat glued to the movie, stuffing their faces. Halfway through, a knock startled them. Canon paused the movie.

Jasen popped to his feet, "Great, I've got to pee." He disappeared.

Canon opened the door. Grammie Nan offered a plate of freshly baked chocolate chip cookies.

Brad sniffed, rising to his feet. "Mm. What a

wonderful scent."

"I thought Canon could share these with his friends." Brad tipped his hat. "Thank you, Nan."

"You're welcome." She handed the plate to Canon. "Thank you all for watching out for Canon. Your friendship is golden." Canon handed Brad the plate, then took Grammie's elbow and walked her the few feet home.

"Thank you. You have great timing." Canon dipped and kissed her cheek.

"Are you having a good time? I hear music. Who's singing?" Grammie asked with a twinkle in her eye.

"That's Forrest. He knows all the words by heart. I guess the movie is one his daughter loves to watch over and over. Or maybe the parents don't hate it as much as the others."

"Heavens, with as much passion as he sings, he loves that movie, too," Grammie Nan laughed. "Have fun and remember, you had a long shift and need your sleep."

"Yes, Ma'am," Canon hugged her. "I love you, Grammie."

"I love you, too."

Canon entered his living room, all eyes trained on him. The plate of cookies lay untouched on the table. Olaf's face, frozen mid-sentence, stared from the screen. "Something wrong with the cookies?" Canon asked.

"No. We are waiting like pigs," Brad informed. "We were afraid to start in on them in case we ate them all."

"Let's make popcorn," Forrest said, hopping to his feet.

"I don't have any." Canon followed him in to the kitchen, stuffing the memory of burning popcorn to the recesses of his mind.

"No worries," Forrest answered. "I brought some. Movie style with all the fake butter. Delish."

Forrest listened to the popcorn while Canon found a few bowls. One made him frown.

"Here." Forrest handed Canon a bag. He shook it, getting one more kernel to pop.

"What's with the long face?" Forrest put another bag in the microwave.

"This was Albie's bowl. It belonged to her grandmother. She treasured it." With a sigh, he dumped the popcorn into it.

"I'm sorry about your girlfriend." Forrest put a hand on Canon's shoulder. "The thing is, once you meet the one, you know. It's weird. All the ones you have beforehand, the not-so-bad ones and the not-so-good ones, teach you what you like or don't like in a relationship."

"What have you learned?" Forrest asked, pulling the other bag out.

"I don't know yet." He tossed popcorn in his mouth. "It's still too fresh." Canon nodded. "When I figure out what went wrong, then I'll be able to process it."

"Take your time, my friend." Forrest threw the empty bags in the trash. "When you're lonely, just ping me or one of the guys. We can always meet you. I love my family, but sometimes I need a little me time, too."

"You can call me anytime," Canon returned Forrest's smile. "When Frozen on Ice comes to a town, I'll go with you."

CHAPTER THIRTEEN

For Sunday night book club, they met at Canon's again. Since they'd swapped books the night of Albie and Canon's breakup intervention and they all read fast, they were ready to switch. Ophelia arrived first, but visited with Grammie Nan before joining the men. They had already selected their new books.

Canon had vacuumed and brought the dinette chairs into the living room.

"What happens in book club stays in book club," B.J. said.

"Are you talking about Disney karaoke?" Ophelia asked from the doorway, holding a plate of cookies.

Forrest covered his tomato-red face with his hands. "How did you—"

"I have my ways." She glanced at Brad and giggled.

"Haven't you noticed she's been in the group chat from the beginning?" Canon pointed out.

"No shit." B.J. rubbed his jaw, appearing constipated. "I, uh, apologize about all that stuff I teased Brad about."

Blushing, Brad crossed his arms over his chest and leaned back. "Let's talk about characterization." He attempted diverting the conversation.

"Nice try." Ophelia patted his knee.

"There's a first time for everything, but B.J. was right about this book. Magic semen is the bomb," Parker said, waving the paperback.

"I'm next in line to read it." Canon said. Parker handed the book over and Canon flipped the novel, reading the back.

"Let's get the series by the author," Ophelia suggested.

The men glanced at each other. "Awesome." B.J. jumped up, thrusting his fist in the air. The others gaped at him. "What? I love the world the author builds. It's kinda like Firefly. You know, alternate earth history. Humans way, way in the future." He put his hands out. "Of course, having a super-wanker is cool."

"Talk about fiction," Ophelia mumbled.

Brad raised his hand. "I enjoyed the world, too. It had rich characters. And even though this was in the middle of the series, I felt it was a standalone. I could sympathize with the non..." he coughed. "Non-super penis individuals. The author painted a picture of the dying race so well you cheer for them."

"Here here," Parker agreed.

Canon opened the book and read the beginning. The first few lines hooked him. Bar fight and damsel in distress. *It's a winner*. When the doorbell rang, it spooked him. He dropped the book.

They glanced at him, and he rose. He hadn't expected anyone else.

Forrest rubbed his hands together. "Maybe Nan made more cookies."

Canon smiled. "It could be." He rushed for the door. A murmuring broke out behind him as the guys and Ophelia sampled the homemade treats.

Canon pulled open the door with a huge smile. His smile dropped when he spotted Albie there. He couldn't breathe.

"You haven't replied to my texts," she whispered.

He rubbed the back of his head, not knowing what to do.

"Let the girl in," Ophelia said.

Canon stepped back, exposing the group to Albie. Her eyes widened, and she blushed, but she continued into the room, pulling her rolling suitcase. She paused alongside the sofa. She raised her hand, wiggling her fingers and offering a gracious smile. "Hello everyone. Book club?"

"Yes." B.J. frowned and crossed his arms.

Ophelia glanced from Canon's pained expression to the other men's hostile glares. "So dear, I'm Ophelia Cox. Have you met the others?"

Albie nodded but still didn't move.

"Did you have a pleasant visit?" Ophelia asked.

"Yes. My dad is going to be fine. Thank you for asking."

"What happened to your dad?" Canon asked. Worry gnawed at his gut. Stepping beside her, he placed a palm on her shoulder.

Albie leaned into his touch. "I told you on the voice

mail."

"No, you didn't. All I heard was that you were leaving me with short notice." His gaze bored into hers.

"Oh, no. I'm sorry, Canon." Albie bit her lip, then heaved a sigh. "The rest of the message about Dad must have cut off." She waved a hand, her blush intensifying. "After we… went to bed, I noticed mom left me a voicemail. She doesn't call that late. Ever. My dad had a diabetic reaction and went to the ER. It was pretty serious."

"Oh, God, I'm sorry." Canon took her in to his arms and hugged her. The sweet scent of her lavender shampoo tantalized his senses.

"It's okay, Canon." She gazed up at him. "You thought I left you?"

His breath caught. "I wondered what I did wrong."

Albie took his face in her hands. "Nothing. You've done nothing wrong. I should have written a note. I'm sorry."

"You aren't leaving forever?" Canon asked.

She snuggled against him. "How can I leave my forever?"

His heart raced, and he turned her around and tipped her chin up. "Do you mean it?"

Albie smiled and nodded. She tiptoed and claimed his lips. Canon gasped, then relaxed into the kiss. His heart hammered, and he heated. Albie's soft warmth pressed against him. She hadn't left him. His heart soared, and he clung to her. She opened for him and his tongue swept in.

She moaned and tightened her hold.

When they ended the kiss, B.J. started clapping. "Great show."

Albie buried her face against Canon's shirt. "Oh," she squeaked, jumping back. "Mr. Doodles is in the car." She raced out and within moments, she let the kitten out of his cat carrier. He darted out and under the sofa.

Canon sunk to the sofa and pulled Albie to his lap. With her hands around his neck, she sighed and said, "Carry on. I'd like to see what happens in this group."

"What happens in book club stays in book club." Forrest said, repeating B.J.'s earlier statement. Albie crossed her heart.

"Well dear," Ophelia said, "we were discussing how the guys love an author who has created an alien with magical sperm. This sperm is so exceptional that any woman they have sex with becomes addicted to it and has the best orgasms of her life."

"Nice fantasy," Albie said.

"Have you read together?" Brad asked.

"Not yet," Albie said. "He wouldn't let me start in the middle. I agree. I'd like to start at the beginning."

"Canon has the magic semen book now. There's a lot of female pleasuring in the scenes," Brad said.

Parker nodded. "Yep. I've read it too. Check out page forty-two. I starred it. Lisa particularly liked that chapter. It might be a winner for you two." He eyed the young couple.

"Do you like ice cream?" Brad asked, winking at

Parker.

"Yes, why?" Albie asked, sitting up.

"Good. It will be fine," Brad said with a chuckle.

Albie leaned back against Canon. Her petite body wasn't heavy, and he enjoyed the pressure against him. He hugged her tight, but after a moment, she sat up straight. "Are those Grammie Nan's cookies?"

"Yes, ma'am" Canon said. Forrest pushed the plate toward her. There were pieces of cookies left. She took one and popped it into her mouth. "Mmm" she hummed.

"So Albie," Jasen said, "You came back to Canon because of his Grammie Nan's cooking."

"No. Because of my B'SHOAF," Albie declared with shining eyes.

"What's that?"

"Me." Canon said. He claimed Albie's lips with renewed fervor.

After they broke apart, Albie said, "He's my big, sexy hunk of a fireman."

"Fire Man, huh?" Jasen teased. "I still think Batman is cooler."

"No way," B.J. said. "Superman and Spider-Man are better. They've got powers."

Parker glanced at Brad, who rolled his eyes.

"I seem to recall Ms. Hardmann saying something about the Fire Man having a magic hose," Forrest reminded, then chuckled.

Laughter filled the room. Even though Canon's face flared hot, he mumbled, "In her dreams."

"Probably," Brad agreed.

Albie whispered, "In mine." She giggled and blushed.

It's one superpower he wouldn't mind using. He tickled her and her laughter rang. Canon figured out his weakness. The sound of her joy and the way her face lit up melted his soul, melding it with hers. Canon gazed longingly into Albie's sparkling eyes.

"I call this dare successful." Forrest clapped his hands and rose.

"I second that motion," B.J. stated.

"All in favor say 'aye'," Jasen added.

Everyone said, "aye." The book club exited the duplex, leaving Canon and Albie alone.

Albie lifted the novel and opened the cover. "Chapter one…" She met Canon's gaze, and they shared a grin.

He dropped to the sofa and patted the cushion beside him. Albie took a seat, tucking her feet under her. He draped an arm around her shoulders as she snuggled against him.

"I can't wait to see my big sexy hunk of a firefighter's interpretation of page forty-two." She raised her hooded gaze and blinked slowly.

Canon's magic hose reacted to her nearness. He squeezed her tight, his heart full. "I'm glad you came back."

"I never left."

Canon set the book aside. With a wolfish grin, he said, "AImee dim the lights."

"Don't you want to read?" Albie squeaked, as he

pulled her onto his lap.

Canon hooked her chin, peering into her bright hazel eyes. "I don't need a book for my happy ever after. I've already found it."

Love a book?

Please leave a review.
Reviews are virtual hugs for
authors

THE FORTUNA DARE SOCIETY

Fortuna Dare Society Book Club for Men.
What happens at book club doesn't necessarily stay
at book club.

BRAD
Book 1

Welcome to Fortuna, Texas where the men are dared to love as big as they live. The men of widower Brad Davidson's book club, the Fortuna Dare Society, are dared to act out a trope, setting, and character with a significant other.

That poses a problem for Brad, who hasn't had a serious relationship in over twenty years.

He likes the town librarian, but it might not amount to anything more than a strange, costume-staged-musically-enhanced meal.

Then again, he married the last woman he went out of his way to date

JASEN
Municipal Liaisons
Fortuna, Texas Book 4

After his wife died in a flash flood, the mayor of Fortuna, Jasen Delay, delved into work. Two years later, he's still wearing the placating smile, but when a vanload of urban consultants visit the town... a beauty catches his eye.

Determined to keep their relationship professional, Jasen and Michaela must stymie their blossoming feelings and focus on revitalizing Fortuna's downtown. A nosy newspaper reporter, a perverted prankster, and sightings of Jasen's wife's ghost have Michaela second guessing her choice to stay. Jasen will do anything to keep Michaela in town. Fortuna needs her but, more importantly, Jasen needs her.

With Jasen's help, can Michaela wade through small town bureaucracy, solve the mystery of the canyon ghost, and learn to trust to her heart? And will Jasen ever fulfill his book club dare?

ALSO BY
ROCHELLE BRADLEY
Romance with Sass & Shenanigans.

The Double D Ranch Book
Plumb Twisted
More Than a Fantasy
Municipal Liaisons
Here We Go Again
The Playboy's Pretend Fiancée
Cole's New Song
Brad
Canon
Destination Escape
The 24 Hour Bet
Love, Lattes, & Holiday Tales

Books by Rochelle Bradley & CJ Warrant
Boba Book Babe Mysteries

Pandemonium in Peoria
Silenced in San Antonio
Holiday Glamping

Magic. Mystique. Mischief.
books by
Rochelle K. Bradley

Dragonfly Wishes - Dragons of Ellehcor 1

Dragunzel - Dragons of Ellehcor 2
Descended - Secrets of the Fallen 1
Charmed by Murphy - The Murphy Brothers 1
Murphy's Paws - The Murphy Brothers 2
The Secret Shelf

ABOUT THE AUTHOR

Born and raised in Cincinnati Ohio, Rochelle developed a love of nature and art. She is a Bearcat, a Buckeye, an interior decorator, and fluent in sarcasm. She currently lives in southwest Ohio and shares her home with a black cat, a leash trained orange tabby, and her Prince.

Rochelle co-hosts (with author CJ Warrant) Wednesday Coffee & Books an Instagram Live show where they interview romance authors. Watch the show Wednesdays at 11 AM EST.

Rochelle is an award-winning author including three IHIBRP (Indie Helping Indies Book Review Project) 5-star awards. *Haunted Memories*, a contemporary romance, won a contest from Ellechor Publishing House. *Against the Laws*, finaled in the Chicago-North's Fire & Ice Contest.

She loves to connect with readers. Scan Rochelle's Linktree (https://linktr.ee/rochellebradley) where you can follow her on TikTok, Facebook, Instagram, and other social media. Visit Rochelle's website to sign up for her newsletter to keep up to date about future novels and book signings: RochelleBradley.com.

www.ingramcontent.com/pod-product-compliance
Lightning Source LLC
Chambersburg PA
CBHW021720190726
48289CB00008B/2614